William Shakespeare's Antony and Cleopatra: A Retelling in Prose

David Bruce

Published by David Bruce, 2022.

This is a work of fiction. Similarities to real people, places, or events are entirely coincidental.

WILLIAM SHAKESPEARE'S ANTONY AND CLEOPATRA: A RETELLING IN PROSE

First edition. July 22, 2022.

Copyright © 2022 David Bruce.

ISBN: 979-8201825843

Written by David Bruce.

Table of Contents

Dedication

Dedicated to Carl Eugene Bruce and Josephine Saturday Bruce

My father, Carl Eugene Bruce, died on 24 October 2013. He used to work for Ohio Power, and at one time, his job was to shut off the electricity of people who had not paid their bills. He sometimes would find a home with an impoverished mother and some children. Instead of shutting off their electricity, he would tell the mother that she needed to pay her bill or soon her electricity would be shut off. He would write on a form that no one was home when he stopped by because if no one was home he did not have to shut off their electricity.

The best good deed that anyone ever did for my father occurred after a storm that knocked down many power lines. He and other linemen worked long hours and got wet and cold. Their feet were freezing because water got into their boots and soaked their socks. Fortunately, a kind woman gave my father and the other linemen dry socks to wear.

My mother, Josephine Saturday Bruce, died on 14 June 2003. She used to work at a store that sold clothing. One day, an impoverished mother with a baby clothed in rags walked into the store and started shoplifting in an interesting way: The mother took the rags off her baby and dressed the infant in new clothing. My mother knew that this mother could not afford to buy the clothing, but she helped the mother dress her baby and then she watched as the mother walked out of the store without paying.

***

The doing of good deeds is important. As a free person, you can choose to live your life as a good person or as a bad person. To be a good person, do good deeds. To be a bad person, do bad deeds. If you do good deeds, you will become good. If you do bad deeds, you will become bad. To become the person you want to be, act as if you already are that kind of person. Each of us chooses what kind of person we will become. To become a good person, do the things a good person does. To become a bad person, do the things a bad person does. The opportunity to take action to become the kind of person you want to be is yours.

Human beings have free will. According to the Babylonian Niddah 16b, whenever a baby is to be conceived, the Lailah (angel in charge of contraception) takes the drop of semen that will result in the conception and asks God, "Sovereign of the Universe, what is going to be the fate of this drop? Will it develop into a robust or into a weak person? An intelligent or a stupid person? A wealthy or a poor person?" The Lailah asks all these questions, but it does not ask, "Will it develop into a righteous or a wicked person?" The answer to that question lies in the decisions to be freely made by the human being that is the result of the conception.

A Buddhist monk visiting a class wrote this on the chalkboard: "EVERYONE WANTS TO SAVE THE WORLD, BUT NO ONE WANTS TO HELP MOM DO THE DISHES." The students laughed, but the monk then said, "Statistically, it's highly unlikely that any of you will ever have the opportunity to run into a burning orphanage and rescue an infant. But, in the smallest gesture of kindness — a warm smile, holding the door for the person behind you, shoveling the driveway of the elderly person next door — you have committed an act of immeasurable profundity, because to each of us, our life is our universe."

In her book titled *I Have Chosen to Stay and Fight*, comedian Margaret Cho writes, "I believe that we get complimentary snack-size portions of the afterlife, and we all receive them in a different way." For Ms. Cho, many of her snack-size portions of the afterlife come in hip hop music. Other people get different snack-size portions of the afterlife, and we all must be on the lookout for them when they come our way. And perhaps doing good deeds and experiencing good deeds are snack-size portions of the afterlife.

Educate Yourself
Read Like A Wolf Eats
Be Excellent to Each Other
Books Then, Books Now, Books Forever

***

In this retelling, as in all my retellings, I have tried to make the work of literature accessible to modern readers who may lack some of the knowledge about mythology, religion, and history that the literary work's contemporary audience had.

Do you know a language other than English? If you do, I give you permission to translate this book, copyright your translation, publish or self-publish it, and keep all the royalties for yourself. (Do give me credit, of course, for the original retelling.)

I would like to see my retellings of classic literature used in schools, so I give permission to the country of Finland (and all other countries) to give copies of this book to all students forever. I also give permission to the state of Texas (and all other states) to give copies of this book to all students forever. I also give permission to all teachers to give copies of this book to all students forever.

Teachers need not actually teach my retellings. Teachers are welcome to give students copies of my books as background material. For example, if they are teaching Homer's *Iliad* and *Odyssey*, teachers are welcome to give students copies of my *Virgil's* Aeneid: *A Retelling in Prose* and tell students, "Here's another ancient epic you may want to read in your spare time."

CAST OF CHARACTERS

MALE CHARACTERS

MARK ANTONY, OCTAVIUS CAESAR, and MARCUS AEMILIUS LEPIDUS: Triumvirs.

SEXTUS POMPEY, son of Pompey the Great.

DOMITIUS ENOBARBUS, VENTIDIUS, EROS, SCARUS, DERCETUS, DEMETRIUS, and PHILO: Friends to Mark Antony.

MAECENAS, AGRIPPA, DOLABELLA, PROCULEIUS, THIDIAS, and GALLUS: Friends to Octavius Caesar.

MENAS, MENECRATES, and VARRIUS: Friends to Sextus Pompey.

TAURUS, Lieutenant General to Octavius Caesar.

CANIDIUS, Lieutenant General to Mark Antony.

SILIUS, an Officer under Ventidius.

EUPHRONIUS, Ambassador from Mark Antony to Octavius Caesar.

ALEXAS, MARDIAN, SELEUCUS, and DIOMEDES: Attendants on Cleopatra.

A Soothsayer.

A Farmer: a comic character.

FEMALE CHARACTERS

CLEOPATRA, Queen of Egypt.

OCTAVIA, sister to Octavius Caesar, and wife to Mark Antony.

CHARMIAN and IRAS, Attendants on Cleopatra.

MINOR CHARACTORS

Officers, Soldiers, Messengers, and other Attendants.

SCENE

In several parts of the Roman Empire.

TIME

The play begins in 40 B.C.E. (Fulvia died that year) when Octavius Caesar is 23 years old, Mark Antony is 43 years old, and Cleopatra is 29 years old. The play ends in 30 B.C.E.

CHAPTER 1

— 1.1 —

In a room in Cleopatra's palace in Alexandria, Egypt, Demetrius and Philo, two followers of Mark Antony, were speaking.

Philo said in response to a comment by Demetrius, "No, but this dotage of Mark Antony, our general, is out of control. His excellent eyes, that over the assembled files and musters of the war have glowed like armed Mars, the god of war, now bend and turn the service and devotion of their view upon a tawny front: the brown face of Cleopatra, Queen of Egypt. His leader's heart, which in the scuffles of great fights has burst the buckles on his breastplate, abandons all restraint, and it has become the bellows and the fan to cool a gypsy's lust."

Gypsies were thought to have come from Egypt.

Trumpets sounded, and Mark Antony and Cleopatra entered. Cleopatra's ladies and servants accompanied her, and eunuchs fanned her. A eunuch is a castrated man — one whose testicles have been removed.

Philo added, quietly, "Look, here they come. Watch Mark Antony carefully, and you shall see in him that the triple pillar of the world has been transformed into a whore's fool. As one of the three Roman triumvirs, Mark Antony rules a third of the world. But despite Mark Antony's power, he has allowed himself to become the fool of Cleopatra. Watch him, and you shall see."

"If it is indeed love that you feel for me, tell me how much," Cleopatra said to Mark Antony.

He replied, "There's beggary in the love that can be reckoned. If I could tell you how much I love you, I would not love you enough."

"I want to know the extent of how far you love me," Cleopatra said.

"Then you must discover a new Heaven and a new Earth," Mark Antony said. "My love for you is infinite and cannot be limited by this Heaven and this Earth."

An attendant entered the room and said to Mark Antony, "News, my good lord, has arrived from Rome."

"This irritates me," Mark Antony said to the attendant.

He then resumed telling Cleopatra how much he loved her: "The sum —."

"No, hear what the ambassadors bringing the message have to say," Cleopatra advised. "Your Roman wife, Fulvia, perhaps is angry at you, or, who knows, perhaps the very young and scarcely bearded Octavius Caesar has used the royal plural and sent his powerful orders to you: 'Do this, or this; conquer that Kingdom, and free this one; perform what we order you to do, or else we damn you.'"

"What, my love!" Mark Antony said.

"Perhaps! Or almost certainly. You must not stay here in Egypt any longer; your dismissal from service in Egypt has come from Octavius Caesar, so therefore hear his orders, Antony. Where are Fulvia's orders for you to return to Rome? Or should I say Caesar's? Both? Call in the Roman ambassadors."

She looked at Mark Antony, whose face was reddening, and said, "As I am Egypt's Queen, you are blushing, Antony; and that blood of yours pays homage to Octavius Caesar and acknowledges that you are his servant, or else your red cheeks show your shame when shrill-tongued Fulvia scolds you. Listen to the ambassadors!"

"Let Rome melt and flow into the Tiber River," Mark Antony said, "and let the well-ordered and vast Roman Empire that arches over the world fall! Here is my space; this is where I belong! Kingdoms are only clay: Our dungy earth feeds beasts as well as men. The nobleness of life is to do thus —"

Mark Antony embraced Cleopatra and then continued, "— when such a mutual pair and couple as we are can do it. I command the world — and I will punish the world if it disobeys — to know that we and our love are without peer."

"This is an excellent falsehood!" Cleopatra said. "Why did he — Mark Antony — marry Fulvia, if he did not love her? I'll pretend to be the fool that I am not; Antony will be himself."

Cleopatra's comment was ambiguous. It could mean that Mark Antony would live up to his reputation of himself as a noble Roman, or it could mean that he would continue to be the fool that he is.

Mark Antony said, "But I will be stirred by Cleopatra."

Mark Antony's comment was ambiguous. It could mean that Cleopatra would stir him to do noble deeds, or that she would move him to do foolish deeds, or that she would stir him to do sexual deeds.

He continued, "Now, for the love of Love — Venus, goddess of sexual passion — and her soft attendants who are called the Hours, let's not waste the time with harsh arguments. There's not a minute of our lives that should pass without some pleasure now. What entertainment shall we have tonight?"

"Listen to what the Roman ambassadors have to say to you," Cleopatra said.

"Damn, wrangling Queen! Everything becomes you and makes you beautiful: chiding, laughing, weeping. Every emotion fully strives to make itself, when you express it, beautiful and admired! I will listen to no messenger but yours, and all alone tonight we'll wander through the streets and watch people. Come, my Queen; you wanted us to do that last night."

He ordered the attendants, "Don't speak to us."

Mark Antony and Cleopatra and their attendants left, leaving Demetrius and Philo alone.

Demetrius asked Philo, "Does Mark Antony regard Octavius Caesar with so little respect that he can ignore his ambassadors?"

"Sir, sometimes Mark Antony is not Mark Antony. He fails to live up to the best parts of what Mark Antony should always be."

"I am very sorry that he proves that common liars, who in Rome spread malicious gossip about him, are speaking the truth, but I will hope for better deeds from him tomorrow. Farewell, and have a good night."

In another room in Cleopatra's palace stood Charmian and Iras, two of Cleopatra's female attendants, and Alexas, one of Cleopatra's male attendants. A soothsayer who predicted fortunes was a short distance away. Charmian, Iras, and Alexas were in a playful mood.

Charmian said, "Lord Alexas, sweet Alexas, most anything Alexas, almost most absolute Alexas, where's the soothsayer whom you praised so highly to the Queen? Oh, I wish that I knew who will be this husband, who, you say, must decorate his cuckold's horns with bridal garlands!"

Alexas had told Charmian that the soothsayer would tell her about her future husband, whoever he would be. He had joked that she would cuckold — be unfaithful to — her husband even before they were married.

Alexas called, "Soothsayer!"

The soothsayer came closer and asked, "What do you want?"

"Is this the man?" Charmian asked Alexas. She then asked the soothsayer, "Is it you, sir, who know things?"

The soothsayer replied, "I can read a little in Nature's infinite book of secrecy."

Alexas said to Charmian, "Show him your hand so that he can read your palm."

Domitius Enobarbus, who served Mark Antony, entered the room and said to some servants, "Bring in the banquet of fruit and sweets quickly; be sure that we have enough wine to drink to Cleopatra's health."

Charmian asked the soothsayer, "Good sir, give me a good fortune."

"I do not make the future; I only foresee it."

"Please, then, foresee my future."

"You shall be yet far fairer — more beautiful — than you are."

Charmian joked, "He means that I will gain a fair amount of flesh and grow fat. Some men like fat women; they are chubby chasers."

Iras joked, "No, he means that you shall use cosmetics when you are old."

"May my wrinkles forbid that! I would rather be wrinkled than use cosmetics!"

Alexas advised them, "Don't vex his prescience the soothsayer; be attentive."

"Hush!" Charmian said.

The soothsayer said to her, "You shall be more loving than beloved."

"I much prefer to heat my body by drinking alcohol than by loving," Charmian said.

"Listen to him," Alexas said.

Charmian said to the soothsayer, "Now predict some excellent future for me! Let me be married to three Kings before noon, and widow all of them. Let me have a child when I am fifty years old to whom King Herod will do homage. Let me marry Octavius Caesar so that I am the equal of my mistress, Queen Cleopatra."

In a few years, King Herod would order many newborn Jewish boys to be killed in an attempt to murder Jesus of Nazareth.

The soothsayer said, "You shall outlive the lady whom you serve."

"Oh, excellent!" Charmian said. "I love long life better than figs."

"You have seen and experienced a fairer former fortune than that which is yet to come."

"Then it is likely that my children shall not have the names of their fathers because my children will be bastards," Charmian joked. "Please tell me how many boys and girls I will have."

"If all of your wishes had a womb, and if all of your wishes were fertile, you would have a million."

The soothsayer was able to joke: He was saying that Charmian had wished to have sex a million times.

"Get out, fool!" Charmian said. "I forgive you for being a witch."

She may have meant that soothsayers, like fools and jesters, have a license to speak freely. Or she may have meant that the soothsayer's skill in forecasting was so poor that no one could ever believe that he was a witch. Or she may have been pretending to be shocked at the soothsayer's comment.

Alexas said to her, "You think only your sheets are privy to your private wishes."

Charmian said to the soothsayer, "Now tell Iras her fortune."

"We all want to know our fortunes," Alexas said.

Enobarbus said, "My fortune and most of our fortunes tonight shall be to go to bed drunk."

Iras showed her palm to the soothsayer and said, "There's a palm that foretells chastity, if nothing else."

Charmian joked, "Even as the overflowing Nile River foretells famine."

An overflowing Nile River actually foretold feast, not famine. The Nile overflowed its banks and irrigated the dry land around it, leading to plentiful crops. Charmian was saying that Iras' palm was moist — this was thought to be a sign of a lecherous person.

Iras replied, "Ha! You wild bedfellow, you cannot soothsay."

"If an oily palm is not a fruitful foretelling of a fruitful womb," Charmian said, "then I cannot scratch my ear."

Charmian then said to the soothsayer, "Please, tell Iras an ordinary, common, workaday fortune."

The soothsayer said, "Your fortunes are alike."

"How are they alike?" Iras said. "Give me some particulars."

"I have already foretold Charmian's future," the soothsayer said. "Your future is the same as hers."

Iras asked, "Am I not an inch of fortune better than she?"

"Well, if you were an inch of fortune better than I, where would you choose it?" Charmian asked.

"Not in my husband's nose."

Iras meant that she would want the extra inch to be in a different spot of her husband's body.

"May the Heavens amend our worser — bawdier — thoughts!" Charmian said.

She then said, "Alexas — come here."

She said to the soothsayer, "Tell his fortune, his fortune!"

She added, "Oh, let him marry a woman who cannot go, sweet Isis, I beseech you!"

Isis is the Egyptian goddess of fertility. A woman who cannot go is a woman who cannot orgasm.

Charmian continued, "And let her die, too, and then give him a worse wife! And let a worser wife follow a worse wife, until the worst of all follows him laughing to his grave, after he has been made a cuckold by fifty wives! Good

Isis, hear and positively answer this prayer of mine, even though you deny me something of more seriousness, good Isis, I beseech you!"

"Amen," Iras said. "Dear goddess, hear that prayer of the people! Just as it is heartbreaking to see a handsome man with an unfaithful wife, so it is a deadly sorrow to behold a foul and ugly knave uncuckolded; therefore, dear Isis, act properly and with decorum, and give him an appropriate fortune!"

"Amen," Charmian said.

Alexas said, "I see now that if it lay in their hands to make me a cuckold, they would do it, even if they would have to make themselves whores!"

Enobarbus said, "Hush! Here comes Mark Antony."

Charmian looked up and said, "It is not he; it is the Queen."

Cleopatra entered the room and asked, "Have you seen my lord, Mark Antony?"

Enobarbus replied, "No, lady."

"Has he been here?"

Charmian replied, "No, madam."

"He was disposed to be merry," Cleopatra said, "but suddenly a Roman thought struck him. He thought seriously about matters in Rome. Enobarbus!"

"Madam?" he replied.

"Seek him, and bring him here," Cleopatra ordered.

Enobarbus left, and then Cleopatra asked, "Where's Alexas?"

"Here, at your service," he replied. "My lord, Mark Antony, is approaching."

Cleopatra changed her mind about seeing him. Using the royal plural, she said, "We will not look upon him. Go with us."

Everyone left the room as Mark Antony, a messenger, and some attendants entered it.

The messenger said, "Fulvia, your wife, first came into the battlefield."

"Was she fighting against Lucius, my brother?" Mark Antony asked.

"Yes," the messenger replied, "but as soon as that war had ended, the situation at the time made them friends and allies. They joined their forces against Octavius Caesar. He had better success and after winning the first battle drove them out of Italy."

"Well, what is the worst news you have brought to me?"

"The nature of bad news infects the teller," the messenger said. "The bearer of bad news is blamed for the bad news he bears."

"That is true when the bad news is given to a fool or a coward," Mark Antony said. "Go on. Things that are past are done with me: What's done is done. This is the way that it is with me: Whoever tells me the truth, although in his tale lies death, I hear him the same way I would if he flattered me."

The messenger replied, "Quintus Labienus — this is stiff news — has, with his Parthian army, conquered parts of Asia around the Euphrates River."

Labienus had supported Marcus Brutus and Caius Cassius, who had assassinated Julius Caesar. He had fought for Brutus and Cassius against Mark Antony and Octavius Caesar in the following civil war. After Mark Antony and Octavius Caesar had defeated Brutus and Cassius, Labienus had gone to Parthia, raised troops, and conquered territory in the Middle East.

The messenger continued, "His conquering banner flies from Syria to Lydia and to Ionia. While —"

The messenger hesitated and Mark Antony said, "While Antony, you would say."

The messenger said, "Oh, my lord!" He was worried about criticizing Mark Antony, who was a powerful man who could have him whipped. Labienus had accomplished all this while Mark Antony had done nothing except party with Cleopatra in Egypt.

"Speak to me straightforwardly," Mark Antony said, "and don't tone down what everyone is saying about me. Call Cleopatra by the names that people in Rome call her. Use the words that Fulvia, my wife, used when she railed against me, and taunt my faults with such full and complete license as both truth and malice have power to utter. Tell me the truth even though you think the truth will make me angry. When our quick minds lie still, then our minds bring forth weeds; but when we tell our faults, then it is as if a field is being plowed in preparation for a future bountiful harvest. When we know our faults, then we can correct them. Fare you well, and leave us for a while."

"I serve you at your noble pleasure," the messenger said and then exited.

Mark Antony called for another messenger, "What is the news from Sicyon — the news? Speak!"

Sicyon, a city in the north of the Peloponnesus in Greece, is where Antony had left his wife, Fulvia.

An attendant asked at the door, "The messenger from Sicyon — is he here?"

Another attendant said to Mark Antony, "He is waiting for your orders."

"Let him appear before me," Mark Antony said.

He then said to himself, "I must break these strong Egyptian fetters, or lose myself in dotage."

Another messenger entered the room.

Mark Antony asked him, "Who are you?"

The messenger replied, "Fulvia, your wife, is dead."

"Where did she die?"

"In Sicyon," the messenger replied. "The length of her sickness, with what else more serious you need to know, is recounted in this document."

He handed Mark Antony a letter.

"Leave me," Mark Antony ordered.

The messenger exited.

Mark Antony said to himself about his late wife, "There's a great spirit gone! Her death is something I desired. What our contempt often hurls from us, later we often wish it were ours again; what is at present a pleasure becomes with the passage of time the opposite of itself. Now that my wife is gone, I value her — she's good. I shoved her away with my hand, but now that hand would like to pluck her back to me. I must break away from this enchanting Queen of Egypt. Ten thousand harms more than the ills I already know about have come into existence because of my idleness."

He then shouted, "Enobarbus!"

Enobarbus, who had stayed nearby in case he was needed, entered the room and said, "What's your pleasure, sir?"

"I must with haste go from here."

"Why, in such circumstances we kill all our women," Enobarbus said. "We see how deadly an unkindness is to them. If they must suffer our departure, then death's the word for them."

"I must be gone."

"Under a compelling occasion, let women die; it would be a pity to cast them away for nothing, although if we must choose between women and a great cause, women should be esteemed as nothing. Cleopatra, if she catches only the least rumor of this departure, will die instantly; I have seen her die twenty times for far poorer reasons. I think there is some life-giving spirit in death — it must commit some loving act upon her since she has such an enthusiastic quickness in dying."

Enobarbus was in part punning. One meaning of the phrase "to die" in this society was "to orgasm." He was saying that Cleopatra had orgasms quickly and often and enthusiastically.

Mark Antony said, "She is cunning past man's thought."

"Alas, sir, no," Enobarbus replied. "Her passions are made of nothing but the finest part of pure love; they are not faked. We cannot call her winds and waters mere sighs and tears; they are greater storms and tempests than almanacs can report. This cannot be cunning in her; if it is, she can make a shower of rain as well as Jupiter, the god who controls thunder and lightning."

"I wish that I had never seen her," Mark Antony said.

"Oh, sir," Enobarbus said, "then you would have left unseen a wonderful piece of work, which not to have been blessed with would have discredited your travel. Travelers are known for bringing back fanciful tales, and many a fanciful tale can be said about Cleopatra."

"Fulvia is dead."

"Sir?"

"Fulvia is dead."

"Fulvia!"

"Dead."

"Why, sir, give the gods a thankful sacrifice," Enobarbus said. "When the deities take the wife of a man from him, they show to the man the tailors of the earth so that they can be comforted. When old garments are worn out, there are members of the tailoring art to make new garments."

Enobarbus was punning again. "Members" could mean members of the tailoring profession, or it could mean male members, aka penises. Old garments wear out, but members of the tailoring profession make new garments. Wives die, but male members create daughters who grow up to become wives. In this society, tailors had a reputation for bawdiness.

Enobarbus continued, "If there were no more women but Fulvia, then you had indeed a cut, and the case to be lamented."

More puns. The word "cut" could refer to the cut of castration. If there were no women other than Fulvia, then with Fulvia's death it would be as if Mark Antony were castrated. The word "case" could refer to a vagina. If there were no women other than Fulvia, then with Fulvia's death Mark Antony would lament the lack of a case.

Enobarbus continued, "This grief is crowned with consolation; your old smock brings forth a new petticoat. Indeed the tears live in an onion that should water this sorrow. Of course, women other than Fulvia exist in the world, and you can replace an old smock with a new petticoat. If tears must be shed over the loss of Fulvia, the tears might as well come from chopping an onion."

"The business Fulvia has broached in the state makes necessary my presence in Rome," Mark Antony said.

Enobarbus replied, "And the business you have broached here cannot be done without you — especially that of Cleopatra's, which wholly depends on your residence here."

Again, Enobarbus was punning. Mark Antony had used "broached" with the meaning "started," but Enobarbus was using it with the meaning "pierced." Mark Antony had pierced Cleopatra in bed.

"No more light and bawdy answers," Mark Antony, who well understood the meaning of Enobarbus' puns, said.

Using the royal plural, Mark Antony said, "Let our officers have notice of what we purpose to do. I shall announce the reason of our quick departure to the Queen and get her permission for us to depart. Not only the death of Fulvia, with other more urgent and important business, strongly urge us to go to Rome, but the letters also of many of our collaborating friends in Rome urge us to return home to Rome. Sextus Pompey, son of the late Pompey the Great, has challenged Octavius Caesar, and Sextus commands the empire of the sea. He controls Sicily, and he has the power to disrupt the importation of grain to Rome and Italy. Our slippery, unreliable, and fickle people, whose love is never given to the people who deserve their love until after the reasons to love those people have passed, begin to give the title of 'Pompey the Great' and all of Pompey the Great's dignities to his son, who, high in name and power, higher than both in blood and spirit and life and energy, presents himself as the greatest soldier. If Sextus Pompey continues the way he is going, he may endanger the whole world."

Mark Antony then referred to a belief of his unscientific age. People had observed that a horsehair placed in stagnant water would seem to move on its own. They believed that the horsehair had become a live worm that would grow into a poisonous snake. Today, we know that the horsehair attracts bacteria that then cause the horsehair to move.

He continued, "Much trouble is breeding, which, like a horsehair placed in stagnant water, has life, but has not yet grown into a poisonous serpent. Tell our men that we must quickly leave Egypt."

"I shall do it," Enobarbus said, and then he exited.

— 1.3 —

In another room of the palace, Cleopatra, Charmian, Iras, and Alexas were talking.

"Where is Mark Antony?" Cleopatra asked.

"I have not seen him recently," Charmian said.

"See where he is, who is with him, and what he is doing," Cleopatra ordered Alexas. "Do not tell him that I sent you. If you find him serious, say I am dancing; if you find him mirthful, tell him that I have suddenly become ill. Do this quickly, and return."

Alexas exited.

"Madam," Charmian said to Cleopatra, "it seems to me that if you love Mark Antony dearly, you are not doing what you ought to make him love you."

"What should I do that I am not doing?" Cleopatra asked.

"In everything give him his way," Charmian replied. "Cross him in nothing."

"That is the advice of a fool," Cleopatra said. "You are teaching me the way to lose him."

"Don't provoke him so much," Charmian said. "I wish that you would be more patient. Remember: In time we hate that which controls us. But here comes Antony."

Mark Antony entered the room.

"I am sick and depressed," Cleopatra said.

"I am sorry to tell you my reason for coming here —" Mark Antony began.

Cleopatra interrupted, "Help me away, dear Charmian; I shall fall. I can't stand this. My body cannot take it."

"Now, my dearest Queen —" Mark Antony said.

"Please, stand further away from me," she replied.

"What's the matter?"

"I know, by the way you are looking at me, that there's some good news. What does the married woman — Fulvia, your wife — say? You may go and return to her. I wish that she had never given you permission to come to Egypt! Let her not say it is I who keep you here. I have no power over you; you belong to her."

"The gods best know —"

"Oh, never has there been a Queen as mightily betrayed as I have been! Yet from the beginning I saw the treasons planted. I knew this day would come."

"Cleopatra —"

"Why should I think you can be mine and true, even though you in swearing shake the throned gods, when you have been false to Fulvia?" Cleopatra complained.

She was referring to oaths made by Jupiter, King of the gods. When he swore an oath, the abode of the gods shook. Even if Mark Antony were to out-swear Jupiter, his oaths were not to be believed — so said Cleopatra.

Cleopatra continued, "It is riotous and extravagant madness to be entangled with those mouth-made vows, which break themselves in the swearing! You make vows with your mouth with no intention to keep them — you break them even as they are leaving your mouth!"

"Most sweet Queen —"

"No, please seek to give me no excuse for your leaving me. Just tell me goodbye, and go. When you begged me to be allowed to stay here, that was the time for words. You did not think of going then."

Using the royal plural, she continued, "Eternity was in our lips and eyes, bliss was in the arch of our eyebrows, none of our body parts was so poor that it was not Heavenly in its origin. Our body parts are Heavenly still, or you, the greatest soldier of the world, have turned into the greatest liar."

"Please, lady!" Mark Antony said.

"I wish I had your inches," Cleopatra said. "Then you would learn that there is courage here."

By "inches," Cleopatra could have meant the inches of Mark Antony's height, or the inches of his penis, or both. She was metaphorically referring to masculine courage.

"Listen to me, Queen," Mark Antony said. "The strong necessity of time commands my services in Rome for a while; but my entire heart will remain here in Egypt with you. Shining swords raised in civil war are besetting Italy. Sextus Pompey approaches the port of Rome. His power is equal to the power of the triumvirs, and when two domestic powers are equal, then quarrels break out over trivial matters.

"People who have been hated, once they have acquired strength, newly acquire love. The condemned Sextus Pompey, rich in his father's honor, creeps quickly into the hearts of people who have not thrived under the present government. The numbers of these discontents threaten the government. Quietness has led to discontent, which having grown sick of rest, wants to purge itself with any desperate change — these discontents want to exchange peace for war.

"My more particular reason for wanting to go to Rome, and that reason for which you should most grant my going, is the death of Fulvia, my wife."

"Although age cannot give me freedom from folly, it does give me freedom from childishness," Cleopatra said. "Can Fulvia be dead?"

"She's dead, my Queen. Look here at this letter, and at your sovereign leisure read about the quarrels she awaked. At the last of the letter, best, you can read about when and where she died."

Mark Antony's use of the word "best" was deliberately ambiguous. He used it to refer to Cleopatra, whom he regarded as the dearest and best — he thought that in some ways she was better than all other women. But he realized that Cleopatra would regard the news of his wife's death as being the best news in the letter.

"Oh, your love for her has been most false! Where are the sacred vials you should fill with sorrowful water? You should fill vials with your tears of mourning so that they can be placed in your late wife's tomb. Now I see, by how you react to Fulvia's death, how you shall react to my death."

"Quarrel no more with me," Mark Antony said, "but be prepared to know the things I intend to do, which I will pursue, or cease to pursue, as you shall tell me. By the fire — the Sun — that dries the mud deposited on the land by the Nile River and makes it ready for planting, I will leave here and act as your soldier-servant; I will make peace or war, whichever you prefer."

Pretending to be about to faint, Cleopatra said, "Cut the laces of my clothing, Charmian, so I can breathe. Come; but no, don't cut the laces. I am quickly ill, and quickly well, depending on whether Antony loves or does not love me."

Mark Antony said, "My precious Queen, stop this. Look at the true evidence of Antony's love for you. It has been honorably tested."

"So Fulvia told me," Cleopatra said sarcastically. She had not literally talked to Fulvia, but was simply saying that she had learned from Fulvia whether Mark Antony could stay true to one woman.

She continued, "Please, turn aside and weep for her, then bid *adieu* to me, and say the tears you shed are shed for me. Be a good actor now, and play one scene of excellent dissembling. Act as if you have perfect honor."

Mark Antony replied, "You'll heat my blood and make me angry. Let me hear no more of this."

"You can act better than this, but this acting of yours is not bad."

"Now, I swear by my sword —"

"And small shield," Cleopatra said.

She said to her servants, "Mark Antony's acting is improving, but this is not his best performance. Look, please, Charmian, at how this Herculean Roman acts in his performance of anger."

Mark Antony claimed to be descended from the Greek hero Hercules, who was super-strong, but who also was a buffoon in old comedies. Some plays were about Hercules' madness that the goddess Juno, who hated him because his father was her cheating husband, caused.

"I'll leave you, lady," Mark Antony said.

"Courteous lord, one word more," Cleopatra said. "Sir, you and I must part, but that's not the word I meant. Sir, you and I have loved, but that's also not the word. I wish I could remember what the word is, but it is obliterated from my memory, and soon I will be obliterated from Antony's memory."

He replied, "If I didn't already know that you are an idle Drama Queen, I would think that you are the personification of idle drama itself."

"It is sweating labor to bear such drama so near the heart as I, Cleopatra, bear this. The pain of separation from you is like the pain of childbirth. But, sir, forgive me; when my attractive features do not appeal to you, they kill me. Your honor calls you away from Egypt; therefore, be deaf to my unpitied folly. And may all the gods go with you! Be the conquering hero! May a laurel wreath of victory sit upon your sword! And may smooth success be strewn before your feet in the form of rushes!"

"Let us go," Mark Antony said. "Come. Our separation so abides, and flies, that you, residing here, go yet with me, and I, hence fleeting, here remain with you. Although we will be separated, a part of you goes with me, and a part of me remains here with you. Away!"

He left.

In a room of Octavius Caesar's house, two of the triumvirs — Octavius and Lepidus — were meeting in the presence of some servants. Octavius Caesar was reading a letter.

He said to Lepidus, "Now you may see, Lepidus, and hereafter know, that it is not Caesar's — my — natural vice to hate our great competitor: Mark Antony. From Alexandria this letter brings the latest news. He fishes, drinks, and wastes the lamps of night in revelry and merry-making. He is not more man-like than Cleopatra; nor is the widowed Queen of Ptolemy more womanly than he. He hardly gave audience to my messengers, preferring almost to ignore them. He has barely remembered that he has partners in the other two triumvirs: us. You shall find in this letter a man who is the epitome of all vices that all men follow."

"I cannot think that enough evils exist to darken all of Mark Antony's goodness," Lepidus replied. "The faults in him seem like the spots — the stars — of Heaven, which are made more fiery by night's blackness. In these troubled times, his faults stand out and are noticed. His faults must be hereditary, rather than acquired. His faults must be what he cannot change, rather than what he chooses."

"You are too indulgent and forgiving," Octavius Caesar said. "Let us grant, for the sake of argument, it is not amiss to tumble on the bed of Ptolemy and commit adultery with Cleopatra; to give a Kingdom in exchange for a joke; to sit and take turns drinking with a slave; to reel and stagger in the streets at noon; and to brawl with knaves who smell of sweat. Let us say that this is suitable for him — although his character must be rare indeed if these things cannot blemish it — yet Antony is guilty of other things. He cannot excuse his failings, not when we bear such a heavy weight of work and responsibility because he plays so delightfully and shirks his duty. If at a different time he filled his idle hours with his riotous living, then he would suffer the illnesses of gluttony and the venereal diseases of lechery and those would be enough punishment — no need for a lecture. But he wastes time that he should gain by ceasing his entertainments — we called him to come to Rome because of our positions as triumvirs. We should chide him as we berate boys, who, although they know better, use their time to pursue immediate pleasure, thereby rebelling against mature judgment."

Seeing a messenger coming toward them, Lepidus said, "Here's more news."

The messenger addressed Octavius Caesar: "Your orders have been carried out; and every hour, most noble Caesar, you will receive news of developments abroad. Sextus Pompey is strong at sea and has many ships, and it appears that those men who have feared but not loved you, Caesar, love him. To the ports these discontented men go, and men say about Pompey that he has been much wronged."

"I expected no less," Octavius Caesar said. "Ever since the first government, we have learned that the man in power was wished-for until he achieved power, and the man who loses power, who was not loved when he had power, is loved after he loses power. The common people are like a drifting reed upon the stream. It goes forward and backward, following the varying ebb and flow of the tide the way a page follows the heels of his master. The reed rots while following the movement of the tide, and the general public wastes its approval by frequently changing the person whom it approves."

The messenger said, "Octavius Caesar, I bring you word that Menecrates and Menas, famous pirates, have taken command of the sea, which serves them, and which they plow and wound with the keels of their ships of every kind. They make many destructive raids on Italy. The people living on the shore turn pale with fear when they think about the pirates, and hotheaded young men revolt and serve them. Each vessel that sails forth is captured as soon as it is seen. The very name of Sextus Pompey causes more destruction than we would have suffered if we had declared war and fought against him."

Octavius Caesar addressed the man whom he wished were present: "Antony, leave your lascivious and lecherous orgies and revelries. In the past, you fought an army led by the consuls Hirtius and Pansa. You killed the consuls, but their army defeated your army, and you and your army were forced away from the city of Modena. At that time, famine followed at your heels. Although you enjoyed an upper-class upbringing, you fought the famine — which not even savages could endure — with patient self-control. You drank the urine of horses, and you drank water from a puddle gilded with iridescent scum — water that beasts would not drink. Your palate then condescended to eat the roughest berry on the rudest hedge. Indeed, like the stag, when snow covers the pasture, you ate bark from the trees. It is reported that on the Alps you ate strange flesh that some people preferred to die rather than eat. All this — your honor now cannot live up to your honor then — you bore so like a soldier that your cheeks did not even get thin."

"It is a pity that Mark Antony is not like that now," Lepidus said.

"Let his shames quickly drive him to Rome," Octavius Caesar said. "It is time we two showed ourselves in the battlefield; and to that end we immediately assemble a council of war. Pompey is thriving while we are idle."

"Tomorrow, Octavius Caesar, I shall be able to inform you correctly which forces by sea and land I am able to assemble to fight this war."

"Until we meet tomorrow, I will be doing the same thing. Farewell."

"Farewell, my lord," Lepidus said. "Whatever you should learn in the meantime of events abroad, please inform me, sir."

"Don't doubt that I will," Octavius Caesar said. "I know that it is my duty."

In Cleopatra's palace in Alexandria, Cleopatra, Charmian, Iras, and the eunuch Mardian were speaking.

Cleopatra said, "Charmian!"

"Madam?"

Cleopatra yawned from boredom and said, "Give me mandragora — a narcotic — to drink."

"Why, madam?"

"So that I might sleep out this great gap of time during which my Antony is away."

"You think about him too much," Charmian said.

"That is treason!" Cleopatra said.

"Madam, I trust that it is not so."

Cleopatra called, "Eunuch! Mardian!"

"What's your Highness' pleasure?" Mardian asked.

"Not now to hear you sing. I take no pleasure in anything a eunuch has. It is well for you that, having been castrated, your thoughts do not fly forth from Egypt as mine do when I think about Antony. Do you have desires?"

"Yes, gracious madam."

"Indeed!"

"Not in deed, madam; for I can do nothing but what indeed is chaste, yet I have strong desires, and I think about what Venus did with Mars."

Venus, goddess of sexual desire, had an affair with Mars, god of war.

Cleopatra said, "Oh, Charmian, where do you think Mark Antony is now? Does he stand, or is he sitting? Or does he walk? Or is he on his horse? Oh, happy horse, to bear the weight of Antony!"

Cleopatra was thinking that she would like to bear the weight of Antony and be ridden by him in bed.

"Do splendidly, horse! Do you know who is riding you? He is half-Atlas of this Earth; he and Octavius Caesar rule the Earth the way that the Titan Atlas holds up the sky. He is the supporting arm and protective helmet of men. He's speaking now, or murmuring, 'Where's my serpent of old Nile?' For that is what he calls me. Now I feed myself with most delicious poison. I am thinking about something I cannot at this moment have.

"Think about me, Antony, who am with Phoebus' amorous pinches black, and wrinkled deep with time. The Sun-god Phoebus Apollo tans me and darkens my skin the way that pinches cause bruises to darken skin, and as I grow older, I acquire wrinkles.

"Julius Caesar with the broad forehead, when you were here above the ground, I was a morsel — a delightful dish — for a monarch, and great Gnaeus Pompey used to stand and anchor his aspect — that is, stare — at my face until he died while looking at that for which he lived."

Gnaeus Pompey was one of the sons of Pompey the Great and the older brother of Sextus Pompey.

Cleopatra's words had an additional sexual meaning. Part of Gnaeus Pompey used to stand up and be anchored in Cleopatra until he "died" — that is, achieved an orgasm.

Returning from Mark Antony, Alexas entered the room.

He said, "Sovereign of Egypt, hail!"

"How much are you unlike Mark Antony!" Cleopatra said. "Yet, because you have come from him, the great medicine has gilded you with its tincture."

The "great medicine" was the philosopher's stone, which was supposed to turn metals of little monetary value into gold and which was supposed to cure disease and prolong life. By associating with Antony, Alexas had acquired a golden tint, according to Cleopatra.

She asked him, "How goes it with my splendid Mark Antony?"

"The last thing he did, dear Queen," Alexas said, "was to kiss — the last of many doubled kisses — this pearl from the orient. His speech sticks in my heart."

"My ear must pluck it from your heart," Cleopatra said.

"'Good friend,' said he, 'say, the firm Roman to the great Queen of Egypt sends this treasure from an oyster. At the Queen's foot, to mend the petty gift, I will add Kingdoms to her opulent throne. Tell her that all the East shall call her mistress.' So he nodded, and soberly did mount a hungry-for-battle steed that neighed so loudly that what I would have spoken was drowned out by the beast."

"Was Antony somber or merry?"

"He was similar to the time of the year between the extremes of hot and cold; he was neither somber nor merry."

"Oh, he has a well-divided disposition! Take notice, good Charmian, it is just like the man, but take notice of him. He was not somber because that would negatively affect the troops who take their mood from his, and for the benefit of those troops he wishes to shine. He was not merry, which seemed to tell them that he remembered his joy that remained in Egypt. Instead, his mood was in between somber and merry — oh, Heavenly mixture! Whether he is somber or merry, either is becoming to him."

She then asked Alexas, "Did you meet my messengers?"

"Yes, madam, I met twenty different messengers. Why do you send so many so quickly?"

"Whoever is born on that day I forget to send a letter to Antony shall die a beggar. Only an event that will cause devastation for many future years can make me forget to write Antony."

She then requested, "Bring me ink and paper, Charmian."

Then she said, "You are welcome here, my good Alexas."

Then she asked, "Charmian, did I ever love Julius Caesar the way that I love Mark Antony?"

"Oh, that splendid Julius Caesar!"

"Be choked if you say another such emphatic sentence! Say, instead, the splendid Antony."

"The valiant Julius Caesar!" Charmian said.

"By Isis, I will give you bloody teeth, if you compare again my man of men with Julius Caesar."

"By your most gracious pardon, I am singing Julius Caesar's praises exactly as you used to sing them."

"I said those things when I was in my salad days, back when I was green in judgment, and cold in blood and sexually immature. But, come, let's go; get me ink and paper. Antony shall have from me every day a different greeting, or I'll unpeople Egypt. I will send Antony a letter each day until Egypt has no more people to carry my letters."

CHAPTER 2

— 2.1 —

Sextus Pompey was meeting with the famous pirates Menecrates and Menas in a room of his house in Sicily.

Sextus Pompey said, "If the great gods are just, they shall assist the deeds of the justest men."

Menecrates said, "Know, worthy Pompey, that although the gods may delay aid, that does not necessarily mean that they are denying aid."

"While we pray to the gods for their aid, the thing that we are praying for is wasting away."

Menecrates replied, "We, who are ignorant, often pray for things that would harm us. The wise powers deny us these things for our good; and so it is a good thing then that they do not grant our prayers."

"I shall do well," Sextus Pompey said. "The people love me, and the sea is mine. My powers are crescent and growing, and my prophetic hope says that my powers will come to the full. Mark Antony in Egypt sits at dinner, and he will make no wars outdoors — all of the 'wars' he fights will be in bed. Octavius Caesar gets money where he loses hearts — his high taxes turn people against him. Lepidus flatters both Octavius Caesar and Mark Antony, and he is flattered by both; but he loves neither of them, and neither of them cares for him."

Menas said, "Octavius Caesar and Lepidus are already engaged in military operations; they rule a mighty strength."

"From whom have you heard this?" Sextus Pompey asked. "It is false."

"From Silvius, sir."

"He is dreaming. I know Octavius Caesar and Lepidus are in Rome together, hoping for Antony. But may all the charms of love, spicy Cleopatra, soften your pale lips! Let witchcraft join with beauty, and let lust join with both! Tie up Mark Antony the libertine in a field of feasts, keep his brain befuddled with alcoholic fumes; may Epicurean cooks sharpen with unsatiating sauce his appetite, so that sleep and feeding may make him forget his honor as if he had drunk from Lethe, the river of forgetfulness in the Underworld!"

Varrius entered the room.

"How are you, Varrius?" Sextus Pompey asked.

"This news that I shall deliver is most certainly true. Mark Antony is expected to be in Rome at any hour. He may be there now because the time since he left Egypt has been long enough for him to make a longer journey."

"I would have been happy to hear less important news," Sextus Pompey replied.

He then said, "Menas, I did not think that this amorous surfeiter would have put on his helmet for such a petty war. His military expertise is twice that of the other two, but let us raise our opinion of ourselves because our actions have plucked the never-lust-wearied Mark Antony from the lap of the widowed Queen of Egypt."

Menas said, "I cannot expect that Octavius Caesar and Mark Antony shall get on well. Antony's late wife committed offences against Caesar, and Antony's brother warred upon Caesar, although, I think, Antony did not encourage him to do so."

"I don't know, Menas, how lesser enmities may give way to greater," Sextus Pompey said. "Were it not that we are opposed to and stand up against them all, it is obvious that they would fight among themselves. They have reasons enough to draw their swords against each other. But how their fear of us may cement and mend their divisions and bind up their petty differences, we do not yet know. Be it as our gods will have it! Now we must fight with our strongest forces to save our lives. Come, Menas."

Enobarbus talked with Lepidus in a room of Lepidus' house in Rome.

Lepidus, who wanted peace between Octavius Caesar and Mark Antony, said, "Good Enobarbus, it will be a worthy deed and shall become you well if you entreat your captain, Mark Antony, to use soft and gentle speech when he meets with Octavius Caesar."

"I shall entreat him to answer like himself," Enobarbus replied. "If Octavius Caesar angers him, let Antony, the taller man, look over Caesar's head and speak as loudly as Mars, god of war. By Jupiter, were I the wearer of Mark Antony's beard, I would not shave it today. I would have it available to be pulled as an act of insult by Octavius Caesar so that I could fight him."

"This is not a time for private and personal quarrels."

"Every time serves for the matter that is then born in it," Enobarbus said. "Every time is suitable for whatever matters arise during that time."

Lepidus said, "Small matters must be set aside for big matters."

"Not if the small come first," Enobarbus replied.

"Your speech is passionate, but please stir no embers up. Here comes the noble Antony."

Mark Antony and Ventidius, engaged in conversation, entered the room.

Enobarbus said, "And over there is Octavius Caesar."

Caesar and his colleagues Maecenas and Agrippa entered the room.

Mark Antony said, "If we settle our disagreements and come to suitable arrangements here, then we can campaign in Parthia. Look, Ventidius."

Octavius Caesar was engaged in conversation: "I do not know, Maecenas; ask Agrippa."

Lepidus, the peacemaker, said, "Noble friends, that which combined us and made us allies was most great and important, and let not a less important action rend us. What's amiss, let's hope that it can be gently heard. When we debate our trivial differences loudly, we commit murder in trying to heal wounds. So then, noble partners, I am asking you earnestly to talk about the sourest points while using the sweetest terms, and I am asking you not to allow bad temper to add to the problems you will talk about."

"You have spoken well," Mark Antony said to Lepidus. "If we were in front of our armies, and ready to fight, I would seek to be reconciled with Octavius Caesar."

Caesar greeted Antony: "Welcome to Rome."

"Thank you."

"Sit," Octavius Caesar said.

"Sit, sir."

"Well, then."

They sat.

"I have learned," Mark Antony said, "that you are taking things ill that are not ill, or if they are, they do not concern you."

"I must be laughed at," Caesar replied, "if, either for nothing or for something unimportant, I should say that I am most offended by you out of everyone in the world. I would be even more of a fool if I should disparage you when I have no reason even to speak about you."

"My being in Egypt, Octavius Caesar, what was that to you?" Mark Antony asked.

"No more than my residing here at Rome might be to you in Egypt; yet, if while you were there, you plotted against my state, your being in Egypt might be my concern."

"What do you mean by plotted against your state?"

"You will understand what I mean when I tell you what befell me here. Your wife and brother made wars against me, and their wars were on your account; you were the reason for the wars."

"You are mistaken," Mark Antony said. "My brother never used my name to justify his war against you. I made inquiries into this, and I have acquired knowledge from some trustworthy sources who drew their swords with you and fought for you. Did my brother not rather flout my authority along with yours, and fight the wars against my wishes? After all, you and I have the same goals and wishes. I have written letters about this to you; previously, my letters satisfied you. If you want to create a quarrel out of bits and pieces, instead of addressing a more serious concern, you must not create a quarrel out of this."

"You praise yourself by laying defects of judgment on me, but you are making your excuses out of bits and pieces."

"That is not so," Mark Antony said. "I know you could not fail to understand — I am certain of it — this necessary thought: I, your partner in the cause against which my brother fought, could not with grateful eyes look favorably upon those wars that threatened my own peace. As for my wife, I wish you had her spirit in a wife of your own. You rule a third of the world, and you control it easily with a light hand, but you could not control such a wife."

Enobarbus said, "I wish that we all had such wives, so that the men might go to wars with the women!"

"My wife was very uncontrollable," Mark Antony said. "The disturbances were caused by her own impatience, but they did not lack some political shrewdness. Grieving, I grant that she caused you too much disquiet. But you must admit I could not stop her."

Octavius Caesar said, "I wrote to you while you were riotously living in Alexandria; you put my letters in your pocket without reading them, and with taunts you forced my messenger to leave your presence."

"Sir, your messenger came into my presence before I gave orders to have him admitted. At that time, I had newly feasted three Kings, and I was not the man that I was in the morning. After the feasting I was drunk, while that morning I was sober. The next day I told him why I had done what I had done, which was as much as to have asked him to pardon me. Let your messenger not be a reason for us to quarrel; if we must quarrel, let's leave him out of it."

Octavius Caesar now began to bring up his most important reason to be angry with Mark Antony: "You have broken the article of your oath; that is something you shall never have tongue to charge me with. When I make an oath, I keep it."

"Go easy, Caesar!" Lepidus said.

"No, Lepidus, let him speak," Mark Antony said. "The honor is sacred that he talks about now — he supposes that I lack honor. But, go on, Caesar; explain the article of my oath."

"To lend me soldiers and aid when I required them, both of which you denied me."

"I neglected to send them to you, rather than denied them to you," Mark Antony said. "That happened when poisoned hours had so incapacitated me that I did not even know who I was or what I was doing."

Caesar thought, *I can guess that the poisoned hours were blind-drunk hours that led to blackouts and incapacitating hangovers.*

Mark Antony continued, "As much as I can, I'll play the penitent to you, but my honesty in playing the penitent shall not make poor my greatness, and my authority shall not be used without honesty."

Caesar thought, *This is an half-assed apology, but it is an admission that he did not send the soldiers and aid that he had sworn to send to me.*

Mark Antony continued, "The truth is that Fulvia, to get me out of Egypt, made wars here. I am indirectly the cause of those wars, and for that I so far ask your pardon as befits my honor to stoop in such a case."

Caesar thought, *This is an half-assed apology, but it is an apology.*

Lepidus said, "Mark Antony has spoken nobly."

Maecenas said, "If it might please both of you to press no further the grievances between you, then you might remember that this present crisis requires that you two work together."

"Worthily spoken, Maecenas," Lepidus said.

Enobarbus said, "Or, if you borrow one another's friendship for the present but not for the future, you may, when you hear no more words about Sextus Pompey, return it again. You shall have time to wrangle with each other when you have nothing else to do. Pretend to be friends until Pompey is defeated, and then return to hating each other."

"You are only a soldier and not a statesman: Speak no more," Mark Antony ordered.

"I had almost forgotten that truth should be silent," Enobarbus replied.

"You wrong this assembly of distinguished people; therefore, speak no more," Mark Antony said.

"So be it," Enobarbus said. "I will be a stone that can think but will not speak."

"I do not much dislike the content, but I do dislike the manner of Enobarbus' speech," Octavius Caesar said, "for it cannot be Mark Antony and I shall remain friends — our characters differ as much as do our actions. Yet if I knew what barrel-hoop should hold us staunchly together, I would pursue it from one edge to the other edge of the world."

Agrippa, one of Octavius Caesar's closest associates, said, "Give me permission to speak, Caesar —"

"Speak, Agrippa."

"You have a sister whom your mother gave birth to. She is the much-admired Octavia," Agrippa said. "And great Mark Antony is a widower now that his wife, Fulvia, is dead."

"Don't say that Mark Antony is a widower," Octavius Caesar said. "If Cleopatra — who most likely considers Antony to be her husband — heard you, she would deservedly reprove your rashness in speaking."

"I am not married, Caesar," Mark Antony said, denying that he was married to Cleopatra. "Let me hear what Agrippa has to say."

"Here is a way for you two triumvirs to be in perpetual amity, to be brothers, and to join your hearts together with an unslipping knot. Let Antony take Octavia to be his wife. Her beauty claims no worse a husband than the best of men; her virtue and general graces reveal qualities that no other woman possesses. With this marriage, all small suspicions, which now seem great, and all great fears, which now carry with them dangers, would then be nothing. Truths would be then regarded as tales, whereas now half-tales are regarded as truths: Unpleasant facts would then be regarded as tall tales, whereas now malicious gossip is regarded as truths. She would love both of you, and this love would make each of you love the other as well as love her. Please pardon what I have said because it is an idea that I have thought seriously about and is not a sudden and impulsive idea. My duty has caused me to think about a solution to your enmity."

Mark Antony asked, "What do you say about this, Caesar?"

Octavius Caesar replied, "Caesar will not speak until he hears what Antony thinks about what has already been spoken."

Mark Antony asked him, "If I would say, 'Agrippa, I agree to marry Octavia,' would Agrippa have the power to bring about the marriage?"

Octavius Caesar replied, "He would have the power of Caesar, and of Caesar's power and influence over Octavia."

Mark Antony said, "The purpose of the marriage is good and fair, and I hope that I may never dream of putting an impediment in the marriage's path."

He said to Octavius Caesar, "Let me have thy hand. Promote this marriage — this act of grace — and from this hour may the hearts of brothers govern our friendship for each other and positively affect our great plans!"

"There is my hand," Octavius Caesar said.

They shook hands.

He continued, "I bequeath to you a sister whom no brother ever loved so dearly as I love her. May she live to join our Kingdoms and our hearts; and may our friendship for each other never again desert us!"

Octavius Caesar was still suspicious of Mark Antony. In this society, people used the words "thee," "thou," and "thy" among intimates. The words "you" and "your" were more formal. Mark Antony had used the intimate "thy" when talking to Caesar, but Caesar had used the formal "you" when talking to Mark Antony.

Lepidus said, "Good! Amen!"

Mark Antony said, "I did not think to draw my sword against Sextus Pompey because he has done unusually great favors for me recently."

When Mark Antony's mother had fled from Italy, Pompey had been a good and considerate host to her in Sicily.

Mark Antony said, "I must thank Sextus Pompey, lest I acquire a reputation for not acknowledging good deeds; once that is done, I can defy him."

Lepidus pointed out that there was no time for that: "Time calls upon us. We must seek and fight Pompey immediately, or else he will seek and fight us."

"Where is he?" Mark Antony asked.

"Near the mountain Misena in the Bay of Naples," Octavius Caesar replied.

"What is his strength by land?"

"Great and increasing," Caesar said, "but he is the absolute master of the sea."

"So it is reported," Mark Antony said. "I wish that we had spoken together earlier! We could have gotten a better start on opposing him and perhaps prevented him from gaining so much power! Now we must make haste. Still, before we put ourselves in arms, we need to dispatch the business — the marriage — we have talked about."

"Very gladly," Octavius Caesar said. "I invite you to visit and see my sister. Immediately, I will lead you there."

"Let us, Lepidus, not lack your company," Mark Antony said.

"Noble Antony, not even sickness would stop me from going with you."

Everyone left except for Enobarbus and Caesar's friends Maecenas and Agrippa. These men were able to speak to each other less formally than the triumvirs had.

"Welcome from Egypt, sir," Maecenas said to Enobarbus.

"You are half the heart of Caesar, worthy Maecenas!" Enobarbus said, implying that Agrippa — the second of Caesar's two great friends, was the other half.

He added, "My honorable friend, Agrippa!"

"Enobarbus, you are a good man!" Agrippa said.

"We have reason to be glad that the problems between Octavius Caesar and Mark Antony are so well resolved," Maecenas said, adding, "You had a good time in Egypt."

"Yes, sir," Enobarbus said. "We shamed the day by sleeping through it, and we made the night light with drinking. We lit lamps to light the night, and the alcohol we drank at night made us light-headed."

Maecenas said, "I have heard that eight wild boars were roasted whole for just one breakfast, and only twelve persons were there. Is this true?"

"This was but as a fly in comparison with an eagle," Enobarbus said. "We had much more monstrous feasts, which worthily deserve to be noted."

"Cleopatra is a very remarkable lady, if the reports about her are true."

"When she first met Mark Antony, she pursed up — pocketed — his heart, upon the river of Cydnus," Enobarbus said.

His words could have had another meaning: When Cleopatra first met Mark Antony on the Cydnus River, she put his "heart" in her "pocket."

"At the Cydnus River she appeared indeed," Agrippa said, "or the person who told me that invented interesting lies about her."

"Let me tell you about that," Enobarbus said. "The barge that Cleopatra sat in was like a polished throne: It seemed to burn on the water because of the reflections of the barge in the water. The poop deck was decorated with sheets of beaten gold. The sails were purple, and they were so perfumed that the winds were lovesick with them. The oars were made of silver, and they stroked the water in rhythm to the tune of flutes, and they made the water that they beat follow faster, as if the water were amorous of their strokes.

"As for Cleopatra's own person, it beggared all description. She lay in her pavilion, which was made of a rich fabric that contained threads of gold. Imagine a work of art depicting Venus, goddess of beauty. Imagine further that the artist's depiction surpasses the real goddess of beauty. Cleopatra was more beautiful than that work of art.

"On each side of her stood pretty dimpled boys, like smiling Cupids, with different-colored fans, whose wind seemed to make glow the delicate cheeks that they cooled, and undid what they had done. The wind from the fans seemed to heat up her cheeks as they cooled her cheeks."

"How excellent for Antony!" Agrippa said.

"Cleopatra's gentlewomen, like the sea-nymphs called the Nereides, like so many mermaids, tended her in the bows and took care of the tackle and ropes, and the knots they made in the ropes were ornaments. At the helm a gentlewoman who resembled a mermaid steered: The silken tackle swelled with the touches of those flower-soft hands that efficiently performed their duty. From the barge a strange invisible perfume hit the senses of the adjacent riverbanks. The city cast her people out so that they could see her; and Antony, enthroned in the marketplace, sat alone, whistling to the air — air that, except that it would cause a vacuum, would have gone to gaze upon Cleopatra, too, and made a gap in nature."

"Cleopatra is an extraordinary Egyptian!" Agrippa said.

"Upon her landing, Antony sent to her and invited her to supper," Enobarbus continued. "She replied that it would be better if he became her guest, and she invited him to supper. Our courteous Antony, who has never said the word 'no' to a woman, after having his hair arranged ten times, went to the feast, and for his 'ordinary' meal pays his heart for what only his eyes eat."

"She is a royal wench!" Agrippa said. "She made great Julius Caesar turn his sword into a plowshare and go to bed. He plowed her, and she bore him a crop: She gave birth to Caesarion, his son."

Enobarbus said, "I saw her once hop forty paces through the public street; having lost her breath, she spoke, and panted. She made what should have been a defect a perfection; her lack of breath spoke for her."

"Now Antony must leave her utterly," Maecenas said.

"Never; he will not," Enobarbus said. "Age cannot wither her, nor custom make stale her infinite variety: other women cloy — sicken with excessive sweetness — the appetites they feed, but she makes hungry where she most satisfies because the vilest things seem becoming in her — the holy priests bless her when she is lecherous."

Maecenas said, "If beauty, wisdom, and modesty can settle the restless heart of Antony, Octavia will be a blessed prize to him."

"Let us go," Agrippa said. "Good Enobarbus, make yourself my guest while you abide here."

"Sir, I humbly thank you," Enobarbus replied.

Standing in a room in Octavius Caesar's house were Mark Antony and Octavius Caesar; Octavia was standing in between them. Some attendants were also present.

Mark Antony said to Octavia, "The world and my great position will sometimes separate me from your bosom."

"All the time that we are separated, I will bow my knees before the gods and pray to them for you."

"Good night, sir," Mark Antony said to Octavius Caesar.

He added, "My Octavia, don't believe what the world reports about my blemishes. I have not kept to the straight and narrow road, but in the future I shall do so. I shall keep to the straight and narrow road as if I had the benefits of a carpenter's square and ruler. Good night, dear lady."

He said again, "Good night, sir."

Octavius Caesar said, "Good night."

Octavius Caesar and Octavia left the room, and a soothsayer entered it.

Mark Antony said to the soothsayer, "I understand that you wish you were in Egypt?"

"I wish that I had never left Egypt and that you had never come to Egypt!"

"If you can, tell me your reason."

"I feel it intuitively, but I do not have the words to describe it; however, you should hurry back to Egypt."

"Tell me," Mark Antony said, "whose fortunes shall rise higher: Octavius Caesar's or mine?"

"Caesar's," the soothsayer said. "Therefore, Antony, do not stay by his side. Your guardian spirit — the spirit that looks after you — is noble, very courageous, and unmatchable, while Caesar's is not; however, when near Caesar, your guardian angel becomes afraid, as if it were overpowered. Therefore, keep space between yourself and Caesar."

"Speak about this no more."

"I will speak about it to none but you; I will say no more, except when I speak to you. If you play with Caesar at any game, you are sure to lose. Because of his natural luck, he beats you even when the odds are against him. Your luster diminishes when he shines nearby you. I say again, your guardian spirit is entirely afraid to govern you while you are near Caesar, but when Caesar is away from you, your guardian spirit is noble."

"Go now," Mark Antony said. "Say to Ventidius that I want to speak to him."

The soothsayer departed.

"Ventidius shall go to Parthia," Mark Antony said. "Whether the soothsayer has occult knowledge or just luck, he is speaking the truth. Even the dice obey Octavius Caesar, and in our sports and entertainments my better ability comes in second to his luck. If we draw lots, Caesar wins. His cocks always win the battle against mine, even when the odds favor my cocks 100 percent to none. His little fighting birds always beat mine in the fighting ring, although the odds are in my favor.

"I will go to Egypt. Although I am making this marriage to Octavia to make peace with Octavius Caesar, my pleasure lies with Cleopatra in the East."

Ventidius entered the room.

Mark Antony said, "Come, Ventidius, you must go to Parthia. Your commission to lead an army there is ready. Follow me, and receive it."

— 2.4 —

In Rome, Lepidus, Maecenas, and Agrippa were speaking about traveling to meet with and fight — if no peace treaty could be made — Sextus Pompey.

Lepidus said to Maecenas and Agrippa, "Trouble yourselves no further. Please, encourage your generals to make haste."

"Sir, Mark Antony will kiss Octavia, and then we'll leave," Agrippa said.

"Until I shall see you in your soldier's clothing, which will become you both, farewell," Lepidus said.

Maecenas said, "I calculate that we will be at Mount Misena in the Bay of Naples before you get there."

"Your road is shorter," Lepidus said. "My plan is to take a longer road. You will reach Mount Misena two days before I do."

"Sir, may you have good success!" Maecenas and Agrippa said.

"Farewell," Lepidus replied.

In a room of Cleopatra's palace in Alexandria, Egypt, Cleopatra, Charmian, Iras, and Alexas were speaking. Some attendants were also present.

Cleopatra, who was moody because she was thinking of the absent Mark Antony, ordered, "Give me some music; music is the moody food of us who engage in love."

The attendants called for music.

Mardian the eunuch entered the room. As a eunuch who had been trained to sing, he had a high but strong voice.

"No, no music," Cleopatra said. "Let's play billiards. Come, Charmian."

"My arm is sore," Charmian said. "You had better play with Mardian."

"A woman can play with a eunuch as well as she can play with a woman," Cleopatra replied.

She asked Mardian, "Come, you'll play with me, sir?"

"As well as I can, madam."

Both Cleopatra and Mardian were giving the word "play" a sexual meaning.

Cleopatra said, "And when good will is shown, though it comes too short, the actor may plead pardon."

Again, some words had sexual meanings. "Will" included the meaning "sexual desire." "Come" included the meaning "orgasm." "Short" included a reference to the size of Mardian's penis. He had been castrated and lost his testicles. He may also have been emasculated and lost his penis.

Cleopatra said, "I'll not play billiards now. Give me my fishing rod; we'll go to the river. There, while music plays in the distance for me, I will catch tawny-finned fishes; my bent hook shall pierce their slimy jaws; and, as I draw them up, I'll think each of them is an Antony, and say, 'Ah, ha! you're caught.'"

Charmian said, "It was funny when you and Antony wagered over who could catch the most fish. You sent a diver into the water to attach a dead, dried, salted fish to Antony's hook, which he fervently drew up."

"That was a funny and good time — one of many we had. I would laugh at him until he lost his patience, and that night I would laugh with him until he regained his patience, and the next morning, before it had reached nine o'clock, I would drink with him until he went to his bed, and then I would put my clothing on him, while I wore the sword he used at the Battle of Philippi where he defeated Brutus and Cassius."

A messenger entered the room.

"I see that you have come from Italy," Cleopatra said to him. "Stuff your fruitful tidings in my ears that for a long time have been barren of news."

"Madam, madam —" the messenger began.

Sensing that the messenger had bad news for her, Cleopatra interrupted, "— Antony is dead! If you say so, villain, you will kill your mistress, but you will receive gold if you tell me that he is well and free, and here you will be able to kiss my bluest veins — a hand that Kings have kissed, and have trembled while kissing."

"First, madam, he is well," the messenger said.

"Why, there's more gold for you," Cleopatra said, "but, sirrah, note that we are accustomed to say that the dead are well. If that is what you mean, the gold I give you I will melt and pour down your ill-uttering throat."

"Good madam, listen to me," the messenger replied.

"Well, go on, I will listen," Cleopatra said. "But there's no goodness in your face. If you are going to tell me that Antony is free and healthy — you have an oddly sour face to trumpet such good tidings! And if Antony is not well, you should come like a Fury crowned with snakes, not like a normal man."

"Will it please you to listen to me?" the messenger asked.

"I have a mind to strike you before you speak," Cleopatra replied. "Yet if you say that Antony lives, is well, and is either friends with Caesar or not captive to him, I'll set you in a shower of gold, and rain rich pearls upon you."

"Madam, he's well."

"Well said."

"And friends with Caesar."

"You are an honest man."

"Caesar and he are greater friends than ever."

"I will make you a rich man."

"But yet, madam —" the messenger said.

Cleopatra said, "I do not like 'But yet.' It takes away from all the good things I previously heard. Damn 'But yet'! 'But yet' is like a jailer who brings forth some monstrous malefactor. Please, friend, pour into my ear all the information you have, the good and bad together: He's friends with Caesar, he is in a state of health, you say; and you say that he is free."

"Free, madam! No. I made no such report. He's bound unto Octavia."

"For what good turn?"

"For the best turn in the bed."

The messenger had used the word "bound" to mean "married," but Cleopatra understood the word to mean "indebted."

"I am pale, Charmian," Cleopatra said.

The messenger said, "Madam, he's married to Octavia, the sister of Octavius Caesar."

"May you contract the most infectious pestilential disease!"

She hit the messenger and knocked him to the floor.

"Good madam, control yourself," the messenger said.

"What did you say to me!" Cleopatra shouted. "Get out of here!"

She hit him again and said, "You are a horrible villain! Get out, or I'll kick your eyes like balls before me; I'll pull out all your hair."

She grabbed his hair and dragged him on the floor while saying, "You shall be whipped with wire, and stewed in a salty brine. Your wounds shall sting in an acidic brine used for pickling."

"Gracious madam," the messenger said, "I who am bringing you the news did not make the match between Antony and Octavia."

"If you say that Antony and Octavia are not married, I will give you a province and make your fortune. The blow that I have already given to you shall make up for your moving me to anger, and I will reward you with whatever gift in addition thy modesty can beg."

"He's married, madam," the messenger said, telling her the truth rather than what she wanted to hear.

"Rogue, you have lived too long," Cleopatra said as she drew a knife.

"I'll run away," the messenger said, looking at the knife. "What do you mean by this, madam? I have done nothing wrong."

He ran from the room and Cleopatra's presence.

"Good madam, keep control of yourself," Charmian said. "The man is innocent."

"Some innocents do not escape the thunderbolt," Cleopatra said. "Let Egypt melt into the Nile River! Let kindly creatures all turn into serpents! Call the slave back here again. Although I am mad, I will not bite him. Call him back here."

"He is afraid to come back," Charmian said.

"I will not hurt him," Cleopatra said.

Charmian exited the room.

Cleopatra looked at her hands and said, "These hands lack nobility because they strike at a man who is lower in status than I am, especially since I myself am the cause of my being so upset. If I did not love Antony so much, I would not be so upset."

Charmian and the messenger came back into the room.

Cleopatra said to the messenger, "Come here, sir. Although it is honest to do so, it is never good to bring bad news. You should give a host of tongues to a gracious message; but let ill tidings tell themselves to the person whom the bad tidings hurt."

"I have done my duty," the messenger replied.

"Is he married?" Cleopatra asked. "I cannot hate you worse than I already do, if you again say, 'Yes.'"

"He's married, madam," the messenger said about Mark Antony.

"May the gods damn you! Do you still say that Antony is married?"

"Should I lie, madam?"

"Oh, I wish you did lie even if half of my Egypt were submerged and made a cistern for scaly snakes! Go, and leave here. Even if you had the face of the very handsome Narcissus, to me you would appear to be very ugly. Is Antony married?"

"I crave your Highness' pardon," the messenger said.

"Is he married?"

"Take no offense against a person who does not wish to offend you," the messenger said. "To punish me for what you make me do seems very unfair. Antony is married to Octavia."

"It's a shame that Antony's fault should make a knave of you," Cleopatra said. "You did not commit the act that you are sure that Antony committed. Get out of here. The 'merchandise' that you have brought from Rome is all too expensive for me. May you be unable to sell it, and in this way may you go bankrupt."

The messenger exited.

Charmian said to Cleopatra, "Your good Highness, have patience."

"In praising Mark Antony, I have dispraised Julius Caesar," Cleopatra said.

"Many times, madam."

"I have paid the price for it now," Cleopatra said. "Lead me from hence. I am ready to faint. Oh, Iras! Charmian! It does not matter."

She ordered, "Go to the messenger, good Alexas. Have him report on the face and figure of Octavia, how old she is, and her personality and character. Don't let him leave out the color of her hair. Come quickly to me and tell me what he says."

Alexas exited.

"Let Antony go out of my life forever — no, let him not go forever. Charmian, although Antony is painted one way like a Gorgon with snakes for hair, painted the other way he is like Mars, the god of war."

She ordered Mardian the eunuch, "Go and tell Alexas to bring me word of how tall Octavia is."

She added, "Pity me, Charmian, but do not speak to me. Lead me to my chamber."

— 2.6 —

In a house near Mount Misena in the Bay of Naples, Sextus Pompey and Menas met with Octavius Caesar, Mark Antony, Lepidus, Enobarbus, and Maecenas. Soldiers on both sides were present.

Pompey said, "I have your hostages, and you have mine, and we shall talk before we fight."

As was customary, the two sides had exchanged important hostages before meeting. After the meeting, both sides would release their hostages at the same time. The hostages ensured the safety of the people in the meeting. Should a person at the meeting be assassinated, the hostages held by that person's side could be killed in retaliation.

Octavius Caesar said, "It is very fitting that first we come to words before we come to blows. Therefore, we have earlier sent to you our written proposal for peace between us. If you have considered our written proposal, let us know if it will restrain your discontented sword. If it will, then you can carry back to Sicily many brave youths who otherwise must perish here."

Sextus Pompey replied, "The three of you alone are the senators who rule this great world, and you three alone are the chief agents for the gods."

One reason for Pompey to oppose the triumvirs was that so much power was concentrated in their hands. Rome had a Senate, but much of the power that used to belong to the Senate now belonged to the triumvirs.

Sextus Pompey continued, "I do not know why my father, Pompey the Great, should lack revengers, since he has a son and friends; after all Julius Caesar, who at Philippi haunted the good Marcus Brutus, saw you there laboring to avenge his death."

Brutus and Cassius, among other Romans, had assassinated Julius Caesar because they believed that he wanted to be crowned King of the Romans. At the Battle of Philippi, the armies of Octavius Caesar and Mark Antony had defeated the armies of Marcus Brutus and Caius Cassius, both of whom committed suicide.

Sextus Pompey's father, Pompey the Great, fought and lost a war to Julius Caesar. Seeking refuge in Egypt, Pompey the Great was assassinated.

Sextus Pompey continued, "What was it that moved pale-faced Caius Cassius to conspire against Julius Caesar; and what made the all-honored, honest Roman Marcus Brutus, with other armed men, who were the courtiers of beauteous freedom, to drench the Capitol with the blood of Julius Caesar, but that they would have one man stay a man and not become a King? And that is what has made me rig my navy, at whose burden the angered ocean foams. With my navy I have intended to scourge the ingratitude that spiteful Rome cast on my noble father."

Pompey was becoming emotionally overwrought, so Octavius Caesar told him, "Take your time."

"You can't make us afraid, Pompey, with your sails," Mark Antony said. "We'll fight against you at sea; on land, you know how much we outnumber you."

Sextus Pompey replied, "On land, you have played funny games with numbers as you did when you bought my father's house for a set sum but did not pay for it. But, since the cuckoo builds not for himself, remain in my father's house as long as you can."

The cuckoo does not build a nest in which to lay its eggs, preferring to lay its eggs in the nests of other birds. Sextus' words to Mark Antony contained a veiled threat: Antony could remain in Sextus' father's house until Sextus forced him to leave.

Lepidus said, "Please tell us — for what you are talking about now is off the subject we should be talking about — how you take the offer we have sent you."

"That's the point we should be talking about," Octavius Caesar said.

"Don't think that we are begging you for peace," Mark Antony said, "but do consider the benefits that you will receive if you make peace with us and accept our proposal."

Octavius Caesar added, "And think about what may follow, if you were to try to get a larger fortune."

One way for Sextus Pompey to try to get a larger fortune than what was offered to him would be to fight the armies of the triumvirs, but of course he might lose. Another possibility for a larger fortune would be to join forces with the triumvirs. He would get now what was promised to him and in the future he might get more.

Sextus Pompey said, "You have offered to give me the islands of Sicily and Sardinia; and in return I must rid all the sea of pirates and send measures of wheat to Rome. If I agree to this, then we can part with the edges of our swords unhacked and with our shields undented."

The triumvirs replied, "That's our offer."

"Know, then," Pompey said, "that I came before you here as a man prepared to take this offer, but Mark Antony made me somewhat angry."

He then explained a reason why he was angry at Antony.

Speaking to Mark Antony, he said, "Although I lose praise of my good deed by telling you about it, you should know that when Octavius Caesar and your brother were at war, your mother came to Sicily and did find her welcome by me friendly."

"I have heard it, Pompey," Mark Antony said, "and I am well prepared to give you the liberal thanks that I owe you."

"Let me have your hand," Pompey said.

They shook hands.

Pompey then said to Antony, "I did not think, sir, to have met you here."

"The beds in the East are soft," Antony said, "and I give thanks to you, who made me return to Rome sooner than I intended, because I have gained by it."

Octavius Caesar said to Sextus Pompey, "Since I saw you last, you have changed."

"Well, I don't know what lines harsh fortune has cast upon my face, but I never let harsh fortune enter my heart and take away my courage."

"This meeting has been fruitful," Lepidus said. "We are well met here."

"I hope so, Lepidus," Sextus Pompey said. "Thus we are agreed. Now I want our agreement to be written and sealed among us."

"That's the next thing to do," Octavius Caesar said.

"We'll feast each other before we part, and let's draw lots to see who shall host the first feast."

"I will host the first feast, Sextus Pompey," Mark Antony said.

"No, Antony, we will draw lots," Sextus Pompey said, "but whether you host the first or the last feast, your fine Egyptian cookery shall receive fame. I have heard that Julius Caesar grew fat with feasting in Egypt."

Julius Caesar had had an affair with Cleopatra — something that Mark Antony was touchy about.

A little angrily, Antony replied, "You have heard much."

"I don't mean anything negative," Pompey said. "I have fair meanings, sir."

"And fair words to them," Mark Antony replied.

Antony may have been sarcastic. In using the phrase "fair words," he may have been thinking about this proverb: "Fair words make me look to my purse."

Pompey said, "Then so much have I heard. And I have heard that Apollodorus carried —"

Enobarbus interrupted, "— say no more about that, but yes, it is true."

"What is true?" Sextus Pompey said.

"Apollodorus carried a certain Queen to Julius Caesar in a mattress," Enobarbus said.

Enobarbus had interrupted because he knew that this was a touchy subject for Mark Antony. Cleopatra had started her affair with Julius Caesar after her loyal follower Apollodorus had smuggled her, wrapped in bedding, into Julius Caesar's presence. Much later, she started her affair with Mark Antony. Enobarbus, however, was plainspoken, and so he had acknowledged the truth of what Pompey had said.

"I recognize you now," Sextus Pompey said to Enobarbus. "How are you, soldier?"

"I am well, and I am likely to continue to do well," Enobarbus replied, "for I see that four feasts are coming."

"Let me shake your hand," Sextus Pompey said. "I have never hated you. I have seen you fight, and I have envied your behavior in battle."

"Sir, I have never personally cared for you much, but I have praised you when you have deserved ten times as much praise as I have given you."

"Enjoy your plainspokenness," Sextus Pompey said. "It becomes you."

He added, "Aboard my galley I invite you all. Will you lead, lords?"

The triumvirs replied, "Show us the way, sir."

"Come," Sextus Pompey said.

Everyone departed except for Menas and Enobarbus.

Menas said to himself, "Sextus Pompey, your father would never have made this treaty."

He then said to Enobarbus, "You and I have known each other, sir. We have met."

"At sea, I think."

"We have met at sea, sir."

"You have done well by water," Enobarbus said.

Menas replied, "And you by land."

"I will praise any man who will praise me, although what I have done by land cannot be denied."

"Nor what I have done by water."

"Yes, there is something you can deny for your own safety," Enobarbus said. "You have been a great thief by sea. You have been a pirate."

"And you have been a great thief by land."

"That I deny," Enobarbus replied, "but give me your hand, Menas."

As they shook hands, Enobarbus joked, "If our eyes had the authority to arrest people, here they might take into custody two thieves whose hands are kissing."

"All men's faces are true, whatever their hands are doing," Menas said.

This is a cynical sentence. It means that all men try to appear to look honest, whether or not they are honest.

The word "true" has more than one meaning. One meaning is "honest"; another meaning is "without makeup."

Enobarbus joked, "But there was never a fair woman who had a true face."

He meant that beautiful women wear makeup, but in order to make a joke Menas understood "true" to mean "honest."

"This is no slander," Menas replied. "Beautiful women steal hearts."

"We came here to fight you," Enobarbus said.

"For my part, I am sorry it has turned into a drinking bout," Menas replied. "Today Sextus Pompey laughs away his fortune."

"If he does, I am sure that he cannot get it back again by weeping."

"You've said the truth, sir," Menas said. "We did not expect to see Mark Antony here. Tell me: Is he married to Cleopatra?"

"Octavius Caesar's sister is named Octavia."

"True, sir; she was the wife of Caius Marcellus."

"But she is now the wife of Mark Antony."

"Really, sir?"

"It is true."

"Then Mark Antony and Octavius Caesar will forever be friends," Menas said.

"If I had to prophesy about this unity between Caesar and Antony, I would not prophesy that they will forever be friends."

Menas said, "I think that this marriage of Antony and Octavia was made more for political reasons than for reasons of love."

"I think so, too," Enobarbus said. "But you shall find that the band that seems to tie Caesar and Antony together as friends will be the very strangler of their friendship: Octavia is of a holy, cold-rather-than-hot, and gentle disposition."

"Who wouldn't want his wife to be like that?" Menas asked.

"A man who does not have that disposition, and that man is Mark Antony. He will go to his Egyptian dish again, and then the sighs of Octavia shall blow the fire up in Octavius Caesar, and as I said before, that which is the strength of their friendship shall prove to be the immediate author of their disunity. Antony will satisfy his lust back in Egypt. He married Octavia only because of political necessity."

"All that you have said is probably correct," Menas said. "Come, sir, will you go aboard Sextus Pompey's vessel? I have a health for you. I want to toast you."

"I shall take the drink you offer, sir," Enobarbus said. "We have used our throats to drink in Egypt."

"Come, let's go."

Music was playing on Sextus Pompey's vessel. Two servants whose job was to serve food talked to each other. They had brought into the room wine, fruit, and desserts. Music was playing.

The first servant said, "Here they'll be, man — on the floor. Some of their plants — the soles of their feet — are ill rooted already: The least wind in the world will blow them down. They are drunk, and they are staggering."

"Lepidus is high-colored," the second servant said. "His face is flushed from drinking too much alcohol."

"They have made him drink alms-drink."

"Whenever their differing dispositions irritate each other, Lepidus cries out, 'No more arguing.' He reconciles them to his entreaty, and then he reconciles himself to drinking all the toasts they propose."

"But it raises the greater war between him and his sobriety."

"Why, this is what it means to have a name in great men's fellowship. Lepidus is by far the weakest of the three triumvirs. I prefer to have a reed that will do me no service as a weapon than to have a two-edged spear I cannot throw."

"To be called into a huge sphere of influence, and not to be seen to have influence in it is similar to a blind man's eye sockets that are empty where the eyes should be. This pitifully ruins the cheeks."

Octavius Caesar, Mark Antony, Lepidus, Sextus Pompey, Agrippa, Maecenas, Enobarbus, Menas, and others entered the room.

In a middle of a conversation, Mark Antony said to Octavius Caesar, "Thus do they, sir: they measure the flow of the Nile River by certain markings on an obelisk; they know, by the height, the lowness, or the mean, if dearth or foison — famine or feast — follow. The higher the Nile swells and floods, the better it is for agriculture. As the flood ebbs, the farmer scatters his grain upon the slime and ooze, and shortly afterward reaps the harvest."

"You've strange serpents there," Lepidus said.

"Yes, Lepidus," Mark Antony replied.

"Your serpent of Egypt is bred now of your mud by the operation of your Sun," Lepidus said. "So is your crocodile."

Lepidus was referring to an outdated and unscientific belief that the Sun's shining on the mud causes the creation of living snakes. He extended this belief to also apply to crocodiles.

"That is true," Mark Antony replied.

"Sit — and drink some wine!" Sextus Pompey said. "Drink a toast to Lepidus!"

"I am not as well as I should be, but I'll never drop out of drinking a toast," Lepidus said.

"Not until you go to sleep," Enobarbus said. "I am afraid that you'll be deep in drink until then."

"Certainly, I have heard the Ptolemies' pyramises are very goodly things," Lepidus said, trying to pronounce the word "pyramids." He added, "Without contradiction, I have heard that."

Menas said quietly to Sextus Pompey, "May I have a word with you?"

Sextus Pompey replied, "Whisper in my ear and tell me."

Menas said quietly, "Leave your seat and let's talk alone, please."

"Not now," Sextus Pompey replied. "Leave me alone for a while."

He said loudly, "Drink this wine in honor of Lepidus!"

Lepidus asked, "What manner of thing is your crocodile?"

Making fun of Lepidus, Mark Antony replied, "It is shaped, sir, like itself; and it is as broad as it has breadth. It is just as high as it is, and it moves with its own organs. It lives by eating that which nourishes it, and once the elements of life are out of it, its soul transmigrates into another animal."

"What color is it?" Lepidus asked.

"It is of its own color, too."

"It is a strange serpent."

"True, it is. And its tears are wet."

Octavius Caesar asked, "Will this description satisfy Lepidus?"

Mark Antony replied, "It will, because of all of the alcohol that Sextus Pompey gave him. If this description does not satisfy Lepidus, he is a complete epicure."

The word "epicure" had two meanings. An epicure is a person who takes pleasure in eating and drinking. Applied to Lepidus in this situation, it meant "glutton for drinking."

Also, the word "epicure" was a play on "Epicurean." The philosopher Epicurus and his followers did not believe in an afterlife and so would not believe in the transmigration of souls.

Menas whispered to Sextus Pompey, who responded, "Damn, sir! Damn! You want to talk to me now! Go away! Do as I order you!"

Sextus Pompey said out loud, "Where's the cup of wine I called for?"

Menas said quietly to Sextus Pompey, "If for the sake of my merit you will listen to me, rise from your stool."

"I think you are mad," Sextus Pompey replied. "What is the matter?"

Sextus Pompey stood up, and he and Menas walked to a place where they could talk privately.

"I have always been a good follower of yours," Menas said. "I have always held my cap off to your fortunes."

In this society, servants and attendants were bareheaded when in the company of those they served.

"You have served me with much faith," Sextus Pompey acknowledged. "What else do you have to say?"

Sextus Pompey said out loud, "Be jolly, lords."

Mark Antony said to Lepidus, who was staggering, "Watch out for the quicksands, Lepidus. Keep off them, for you are sinking."

Menas said to Sextus Pompey, "Would you like to be lord of all the world?"

"What are you saying?"

"Would you like to be lord of all the world? That's the second time I said it."

"How can that ever happen?"

"Entertain the thought in your mind," Menas said, "and although you think that I am poor, I am the man who will give you all the world."

"Have you drunk well tonight?" Sextus Pompey asked.

"No, Sextus Pompey, I have kept myself away from the cup. You are, if you dare to be, the Earthly Jove. The god Jove is the ruler of the sky; you can be the ruler of the Earth. Whatever the ocean fences in, or the sky embraces, is yours, if you will have it."

"Show me the way this is possible," Sextus Pompey said.

"These three world-sharers, these competitors and associates, these triumvirs are in your vessel. Let me cut the anchor cable, and when we are away from shore, I will cut their throats. Everything then is yours."

"All this you should have done, and not have spoken to me about it ahead of time!" Sextus Pompey said. "For me to do that would be villainous. For you to have done that would have been good service. You must know that it is not my profit that leads my honor; rather, my honor leads my profit. To me, honor is more important than profit. Repent that your tongue has so betrayed your act. If you had done this without my knowing about it, I would afterwards have thought it well done, but now I must condemn it. Think no more about doing this, and drink."

Sextus Pompey returned to the others.

Alone, Menas said to himself, "Because of this, I'll never follow your weakened fortunes any more. Whoever seeks something, and will not take it when once it is offered, shall never find it again."

Sextus Pompey said loudly, "Drink to the health of Lepidus!"

"He is unconscious. Carry him ashore," Mark Antony said. "I'll drink it for him, Sextus Pompey."

Whenever someone was toasted, that person was obligated to drink a full cup of wine. Because Lepidus was incapacitated, Antony drank the wine for him.

Enobarbus said, "Here's to you, Menas!"

"Enobarbus, welcome!" Menas replied.

Sextus Pompey said, "Fill the cup until it overflows."

Enobarbus pointed to the attendant who was carrying off Lepidus and said, "There's a strong fellow, Menas."

"Why do you think so?"

"He is carrying the third part of the world, man. Do you see it? He is carrying off a triumvir who rules a third of the world."

"The third part, then, is drunk. I wish that all of the world were drunk so that it might go on wheels and spin quickly!"

"Drink up," Enobarbus said. "By drinking, you can increase your own giddiness and spinning."

"Come, let's drink," Menas said.

"This is not yet an Alexandrian feast," Sextus Pompey said.

He was referring to Cleopatra's feasts in Alexandria, Egypt.

"It ripens towards it," Mark Antony said. "Clink the cups against each other. Here's to Caesar!"

"I could well do without another toast," Octavius Caesar said. "This is an unnatural labor. I wash my brain with alcohol, and it grows fouler."

"Be a child of the time," Mark Antony said. "Enjoy the party."

"Drink your cup," Caesar said. "I'll answer by drinking mine. But I had rather fast from everything for four days than drink so much in one day."

Enobarbus said to Mark Antony, "My brave Emperor, shall we dance now the Egyptian Bacchanals, and celebrate our wine?"

"Let's do it, good soldier," Sextus Pompey said.

"Come, let's all take hands and dance until the conquering wine has steeped our senses in the soft and delicate Lethe, the river of forgetfulness."

"Everybody, take hands," Enobarbus said. "Make an assault against our ears with the loud music. I will put you where you will stand for dancing, and then the boy shall sing. The refrain every man shall sing as loud as his strong sides can volley."

Music played, and Enobarbus made sure that everyone was in the proper position.

A boy sang this song:

"*Come, you monarch of the vine,*

"*Plump Bacchus with pink, half-closed eyes!*

"*In your vats our cares be drowned,*

"*With your grapes our hair be crowned.*"

Everybody sang the chorus:

"*Fill our cups, until the world spins round,*

"*Fill our cups, until the world spins round!*"

"What more can anyone wish for tonight?" Octavius Caesar said. "Sextus Pompey, good night. Mark Antony, you good brother-in-law, let me request that we leave the vessel and go on shore. Our graver and more serious business frowns at this levity. Gentle lords, let's part. You see that we have burnt our cheeks — our faces are flushed from the alcohol we have drunk. Strong Enobarbus is weaker than the wine; and my own tongue slurs what it speaks. This wild and disorderly performance has almost made fools of us all. I don't need to say anything more. Good night. Good Antony, give me your hand."

They shook hands.

Sextus Pompey said to Mark Antony, "We'll have a drinking match on shore."

"We shall, sir," Mark Antony replied. "Give me your hand."

"Antony, you have my father's house, but so what? We are friends," the drunk Sextus Pompey said, adding, "Come, everyone, I will show you the way down into the boat."

Enobarbus advised, "Be careful that you don't fall."

Everyone departed except for Enobarbus and Menas.

Enobarbus said, "Menas, I won't go on shore."

"No," Menas said. "Go to my cabin."

He ordered the musicians, "These drums! These trumpets! Flutes! Let Neptune hear us bid a loud farewell to these great fellows who are leaving. Make music and be hanged — make your music loud!"

The music played loudly.

Enobarbus tossed his cap into the air and yelled, "Yahoo! There's my cap."

"Yahoo!" Menas yelled, and then he said, "Noble captain, come with me."

CHAPTER 3

— 3.1 —

On a plain in Syria, Ventidius stood. He had triumphed in carrying out the orders that Mark Antony had given him and had won the battle against the Parthians. He had killed Pacorus, an important enemy, and his soldiers were carrying the dead body. Many soldiers were present as Ventidius spoke with Silius, an officer who served him.

Ventidius said, "Now, darting Parthia, you are struck; and now Fortune has been pleased to make me the revenger of Marcus Crassus' death. Bear the King's son's body before our army. King Orodes, Pacorus, who is your son, pays with his death for the death of Marcus Crassus."

The Parthians' cavalry was feared. The Parthian warriors would throw spears at the enemy, and then ride away, seemingly in retreat, but they were able to shoot arrows at the enemy as they rode away. The Parthians could dart on their horses, and their spears and arrows were called darts.

The Romans had borne a grudge against the Parthians because the Parthians had succeeded in defeating and killing Marcus Crassus, one of the members of the First Triumvirate; the other members were Pompey the Great and Julius Caesar. Ventidius had avenged that death by killing in battle Pacorus, the son of Orodes, the King of the Parthians.

Silius, an officer who served Ventidius, said to him, "Noble Ventidius, while your sword is still warm with Parthian blood, pursue the fugitive Parthians; spur your horses through Media, Mesopotamia, and the shelters where the routed Parthians fly. That way, your grand captain Antony shall set you on triumphant chariots and put garlands on your head."

"Oh, Silius, Silius," Ventidius replied, "I have done enough; a person of a lower rank, note well, may do too great an act: Such a person can be too successful. Learn this, Silius: It is better to leave something undone, than by our deed acquire too much fame when the man we serve is away. Both Octavius Caesar and Mark Antony have always won more in their officers than in their own person: Their officers earn most of the victories of the men they serve. Sossius, who was one of my rank who served in Syria, and who was Mark

Antony's lieutenant, because he quickly accumulated renown, which he achieved by the minute, lost Antony's favor. Who does in the wars more than his captain can becomes his captain's captain, and ambition, the soldier's virtue, chooses to lose rather than gain that which darkens him. It is better to lose a battle than to gain a victory that will harm one's career. I could do more to do Antony good, but my success would offend him, and because my success would offend him, I would get no benefit from my success."

Ventidius was afraid that if he accomplished more than Mark Antony in war, then Mark Antony would hurt Ventidius' military career. Mark Antony would not want Ventidius to become Mark Antony's captain.

Silius said, "You have, Ventidius, that quality of discretion without which a soldier, and his sword, can scarcely be distinguished. What will you write to Antony?"

"I'll humbly tell him what we have accomplished in his name, that magical word of war. I will tell him how, with his banners and his well-paid soldiers, we have jaded out of the battlefield the never-before-beaten cavalry of Parthia."

Ventidius was punning with the word "jade." A jade was a broken-down horse, and "to jade" meant "to exhaust."

"Where is Mark Antony now?"

"He intends to go to Athens, Greece, where, with what haste the weight — the supply train — we must convey with us will permit, we shall appear before him. Let's go! Pass the word to the soldiers!"

Agrippa, who served Octavius Caesar, and Enobarbus, who served Mark Antony, talked together in an antechamber in the house where Octavius Caesar was staying.

Agrippa asked, "What, are the brothers parted?"

He was referring to Sextus Pompey and the three triumvirs — Caesar, Antony, and Lepidus — who had been celebrating the peace treaty with feasts and drunkenness.

Enobarbus replied, "They have finished their business with Sextus Pompey. He has gone; the other three are sealing their copies of the peace treaty. Octavia weeps because she must leave Rome. Caesar is sad and serious; and Lepidus, since Sextus Pompey's feast, as Menas says, is troubled with the greensickness."

The greensickness was an anemic condition suffered by young teenaged girls, and people thought that lovesickness caused it. Enobarbus was calling Lepidus' hangover the greensickness because Lepidus was known for very highly praising his fellow triumvirs.

"It is a noble Lepidus," Agrippa said.

"A very fine and elegant one," Enobarbus said.

He was engaging in wordplay. In Latin, *lepidus* meant *fine* and *elegant*.

He added, "Oh, how he loves Caesar!"

"How dearly he adores Mark Antony!" Agrippa said.

"Caesar? Why, he's the Jupiter of men!"

"What's Antony? The god of Jupiter!"

"Did you speak of Caesar? Wow! The nonpareil! He has no equal!" Enobarbus said.

"Oh, Antony! Oh, you Arabian bird!"

The Arabian bird was the mythological Phoenix. Only one existed at a time, and when it grew old, it burned and then a young bird arose out of the ashes.

"If you want to praise Caesar, say 'Caesar,'" Enobarbus said. "You need say nothing more. No praise is higher than that!"

"Indeed, Lepidus plied them both with excellent praises," Agrippa said.

"But he loves Caesar best; yet he loves Antony," Enobarbus said. "Hearts cannot think, tongues cannot speak, numbers cannot calculate, scribes cannot write, bards cannot sing, poets cannot make verses that will adequately describe Lepidus' love for Antony. But as for Lepidus' love for Caesar, kneel down, kneel down, and wonder."

"Lepidus loves Caesar and Antony."

"They are his wings, and he is their beetle," Enobarbus said.

Trumpets sounded, and he added, "This is the sign that soon we must mount our horses and leave. *Adieu*, noble Agrippa."

"May you have good fortune, worthy soldier; and farewell."

Octavius Caesar, Mark Antony, Lepidus, and Octavia entered the room.

"You need make that point no further, sir," Mark Antony said to Octavius Caesar.

"You take from me a great part of myself," Caesar replied, referring to Octavia, his sister, whom Antony had married. "Treat me well by treating my sister well."

He added, "Sister, prove to be such a wife as I think you are — I would give my utmost bond that you will be a good and honorable wife."

He then said, "Most noble Antony, let not this masterpiece of virtue, who is set between us as the cement of our friendship to keep it strong, be the ram to batter at its fortress, for we might better have been friendly without this means of forming an alliance, if on both parts Octavia is not cherished."

"Don't offend me by your mistrust," Mark Antony replied.

"I mean what I said," Octavius Caesar said.

"You shall not find, even if you search for it, the least cause for what you seem to fear, so may the gods keep you safe, and make the hearts of Romans serve your ends! We will here part."

"Farewell, my dearest sister; may you fare well," Caesar said to Octavia. "May the elements be kind to you, and your spirits be all of comfort! Fare you well."

"My noble brother!" Octavia said.

She wept.

"The April is in her eyes: It is love's spring, and these showers of tears bring it on," Mark Antony said. "Be cheerful."

Octavia said to her brother, "Sir, look well after my husband's house; and ..."

She hesitated.

"What, Octavia?" Caesar asked.

"I'll whisper it to you."

Octavia had been previously married, but she had been widowed, and she wanted her brother to look after the house of her first husband.

Antony said to himself, "Her tongue will not obey her heart, nor can her heart inform her tongue. Her tongue is like a feather of a swan's down that stands still upon the swell at full tide. The tide neither ebbs nor flows, and so the feather stands still. Octavia's loyalties are divided between her brother and her husband, and neither is stronger than the other."

Enobarbus and Agrippa spoke together quietly.

Enobarbus said, "Is Caesar going to cry?"

"It looks like it. He has a cloud in his face."

"He would be the worse for that, if he were a horse: A dark spot on the face of a horse lowers the value of the horse. Caesar being a man, the cloud lowers his value: Men ought not to cry."

Agrippa replied, "Why, Enobarbus, when Antony found Julius Caesar dead, he cried almost to roaring; and he wept when at Philippi he found Brutus slain."

"That year, indeed, he was troubled with a rheum that made his eyes water. What he killed willingly in wartime, he wailed — believe it — until I wept, too."

Caesar said, "No, sweet Octavia. You shall hear from me continually. The time shall not outrace my thinking about you — I will always be thinking about you."

"Come, sir, come; I'll wrestle with you in my strength of friendship for you," Antony said.

He embraced Caesar and said, "Look, here I have you; now I let you go, and I give you to the gods."

Caesar said, "*Adieu*; be happy!"

Lepidus said, "Let all the numerous stars light your fair way!"

"Farewell, farewell!" Caesar said.

He kissed his sister.

"Farewell!" Mark Antony said.

In a room in Cleopatra's palace in Alexandria, Egypt, Cleopatra, Charmian, Iras, and Alexas were speaking.

"Where is the fellow — the messenger I beat?" Cleopatra asked.

"Half afraid to come," Alexas replied.

"Nonsense," Cleopatra said. "Nonsense."

The messenger whom Cleopatra had previously beaten entered the room.

"Come here, sir," she said to him.

Alexas said, "Good majesty, King Herod of Judea dare not look upon you except when you are well pleased."

"I'll have that Herod's head, but how can I get it, when Antony is gone? If Antony were here, I could have him get me Herod's head," Cleopatra said.

She ordered the messenger, "Come near me."

"Most gracious majesty —" the messenger began.

"Did you see Octavia?" Cleopatra asked.

"Yes, dread Queen."

"Where?"

"Madam, in Rome. I looked her in the face, and saw her led between her brother and Mark Antony."

"Is she as tall as me?"

"She is not, madam."

"Did you hear her speak? Is she shrill-tongued or low-voiced?"

"Madam, I heard her speak; she is low-voiced."

"That's not so good for her; Mark Antony cannot like her long."

"Like her!" Charmian, who was loyal to Cleopatra, said. "Oh, Isis! That is impossible."

"I think so, too, Charmian," Cleopatra said. "Octavia is dull of tongue, and dwarfish!"

She asked the messenger, "What majesty is in her gait? Remember, if ever you looked on majesty. You know what a majestic walk is!"

"She creeps," the messenger said. "Her motion and her standing still are similar. She shows a body rather than a life; she seems to be more dead than alive; she seems to be a statue more than a living, breathing person."

"Is this true?"

"If it isn't, then I have no powers of observation."

Charmian said, "Not three people in Egypt have better powers of observation than this messenger."

Cleopatra said, "He's very knowledgeable; I do perceive it. There's nothing for me to be worried about in Octavia yet. The fellow has good judgment."

"He has excellent judgment," Charmian said.

"Guess how old she is, please," Cleopatra said to the messenger.

"Madam, she was a widow —"

"Widow! Charmian, do you hear that!"

"And I do think she's thirty," the messenger said.

Antony married Octavia in 40 B.C.E., when Cleopatra was twenty-nine years old. The pact of Misenum between Sextus Pompey and the three triumvirs occurred in 39 B.C.E., when Cleopatra was thirty years old. Both Octavia and Cleopatra were possibly born in the same year: 69 B.C.E. Historians think that Octavia was born between 69 and 66 B.C.E.

"Do you remember her face? Is it long or round?" Cleopatra asked.

"Round even to faultiness."

"For the most part, too, people who have round faces are foolish," Cleopatra said. "Her hair, what is its color?"

"Brown, madam: and her forehead is as low as she would wish it."

This was a way of saying that she had a low forehead and would not wish it to be lower. In this society, high foreheads were valued.

"There's gold for you," Cleopatra said, giving the messenger money. "You must not take my former sharpness with you ill. I will employ you to go back to Antony again. I find you very suitable for that business. Go and prepare to travel; our letters are prepared for you to deliver them."

The messenger exited.

"He is a proper and excellent man," Charmian said.

"Indeed, he is," Cleopatra said. "I much repent that I so harried him. Why, I think, based on what he said, this creature Octavia is nothing for me to worry about."

"She is nothing, madam," Charmian said.

"The man has seen some majesty, and he should know."

"Has he seen majesty?" Charmian said. "Isis forbid that he should say otherwise! He has served you so long!"

"I have one thing more to ask him yet, good Charmian," Cleopatra said, "but it is not important. You shall bring him to me where I will write. All may be well enough."

"I assure you that all will be well, madam," Charmian said.

In a room in Mark Antony's house in Athens, Greece, Antony and Octavia were speaking.

Mark Antony complained, "No, no, Octavia, not only that — that is excusable, that, and thousands more of similar importance — but Octavius Caesar has waged new wars against Sextus Pompey. Caesar also made his will, and read it aloud to the public, no doubt to gain the public's favor by leaving the citizens good things. He has spoken only scantly of me. When he could not avoid praising me, he spoke his praise coldly and sickly. He has given me very little praise and credit. When he had the opportunity to praise me publicly, he spoke that praise only grudgingly."

Octavia replied, "Oh, my good lord, don't believe all you hear, or if you must believe it, don't resent all you hear. If you and my brother should quarrel, an unhappier lady has never stood between two parties, praying for both. The good gods will mock and laugh at me when I pray, 'Oh, bless my lord and husband!' and undo that prayer by crying out as loudly, 'Oh, bless my brother!' When I pray that my husband wins, and I pray that my brother wins, I destroy my prayers because my prayers are contradictory. There is no middle ground at all between these opposing prayers."

"Gentle Octavia, let your best love support the side that seeks best to preserve your love and support you," Mark Antony said. "If I lose my honor, I lose myself. It would be better if I were not yours than to be yours so branchless — so pruned of honor. But, as you requested, you shall go and try to make peace between your brother and me. In the meantime, lady, I'll raise the preparation of an army that shall eclipse that of your brother. Make your soonest haste; this is something you want to do."

"Thank you, my lord," Octavia said. "May the Jove of power make me, who am most weak, the reconciler of my brother and you! A war between you two would be as if the world should be split in two and slain men thrown into the rift to fill it up."

"When you learn who is responsible for this rift, turn your displeasure that way — be angry at that person," Mark Antony said. "My faults and your brother's faults can never be so equal that your love can equally move with them. You must be angry at one of us. Provide for your journey. Choose your own company, and spend whatever amount of money you want to."

— 3.5 —

In a room of Mark Antony's house in Athens, Greece, Enobarbus and Eros, one of Mark Antony's friends, spoke.

"How are you, friend Eros?"

"There's strange news come, sir."

"What news, man?"

"Octavius Caesar and Lepidus have made war upon Sextus Pompey."

"That is old news. What is the outcome? Who won?"

"Octavius Caesar, having made use of Lepidus in the war against Sextus Pompey, immediately denied him partnership and equality; Caesar would not let Lepidus partake in the glory of the action. Not satisfied with that insult, Caesar accused Lepidus of treachery in letters that Lepidus had formerly written to Sextus Pompey. Upon Caesar's own charge and with no other evidence, Caesar arrested Lepidus. The weakest triumvir is shut up in prison until death frees him."

Enobarbus replied, "Then, world, you have a pair of jaws, and no more. And if you throw between them all the food you have, they'll grind the one against the other. Caesar and Antony will come to blows; they will make war against each other. Where's Antony?"

"He's walking in the garden, and he kicks the rushes that lie before him, like this" — Eros imitated an angry Antony. "He cries, 'Lepidus, you are a fool!' — and he threatens to cut the throat of his officer who murdered Sextus Pompey."

"Our great navy's rigged and ready to sail," Domitius Enobarbus said.

"To Italy and Caesar," Eros said. "I have more to say, Domitius, but Antony, my lord, wants to see you immediately. I should have told you my news later."

"My being a minute late won't matter. So be it. Take me to Antony."

"Come, sir."

In a room in Octavius Caesar's house in Rome, Caesar, Agrippa, and Maecenas were speaking.

"Contemptuous of Rome, Mark Antony has done all this, and more, in Alexandria, Egypt. Here's what he did. In the marketplace, on a silvered platform, Cleopatra and Antony were publicly enthroned in chairs of gold. At their feet sat Caesarion, whom they call my father's son."

Octavius Caesar was the great-nephew of Julius Caesar, but Julius had adopted Octavius as his son. Caesarion was reputed to be Julius Caesar's son by Cleopatra.

Octavius added, "Also sitting at their feet were all the illegitimate children that the lust of Antony and Cleopatra has made between them. To her he gave the confirmed possession of Egypt; he also made her absolute Queen of lower Syria, Cyprus, and Lydia."

"He did all this in the public eye?" Maecenas asked.

"In the public ground for shows," Octavius Caesar replied. "His sons he there proclaimed the Kings of Kings. He gave to Alexander great Media, Parthia, and Armenia. To Ptolemy he assigned Syria, Cilicia, and Phoenicia. Cleopatra that day appeared wearing the attire of the goddess Isis. She has often appeared dressed that way when she gives audience — so it is reported."

"Let Rome be thus informed," Maecenas said. "The Romans should know about this."

"The Roman people, who are already sick of Antony's insolence, will cease to think well of him," Agrippa said.

"The Roman people already know about his actions; and they have now received Antony's accusations."

"Whom does he accuse?"

"Me, Caesar. He charges that, once we defeated Sextus Pompey and took Sicily as our spoils, we did not give him his part of the island of Sicily. He also says that he lent me some ships that I did not return to him. Lastly, he frets that Lepidus has been deposed from the triumvirate and that we keep all of Lepidus' revenue."

"Sir, these charges should be answered," Agrippa advised.

"My reply has already been written," Octavius Caesar said, "and the messenger has gone to deliver it to Mark Antony. I have told him that Lepidus had grown too cruel and had abused his high authority, and therefore he deserved his change of fortune from triumvir to prisoner. As for what I have conquered, I am willing to grant him part, but in turn I demand part of Armenia and the other Kingdoms he has conquered."

"He'll never agree to that," Maecenas said.

"Then we will not agree to give him part of Sicily," Caesar replied.

Octavia and a train of attendants entered the room.

She said to her brother, "Hail, Caesar, and my lord! Hail, most dear Caesar!"

"It's a pity that I should ever call you cast away — rejected and discarded!" Octavius Caesar said.

"You have never called me that before, nor do you have cause to call me that now."

"Why have you stolen upon us like this!" Octavius Caesar said. "We did not expect you! You came here not like Caesar's sister should. The wife of Mark Antony should have an army for an escort, and the neighs of horses should give notice of her approach long before she appears. The trees by the road should have been full of men waiting to see you. People should grow faint as they wait and long to see you. Indeed, the dust raised by the many troops escorting you should have ascended to the roof of Heaven, but instead you have come to Rome like a maiden going to the marketplace. You have forestalled us from showing you our love for you with a great public display. Without such a public display, people may think that I do not love you. If we had known you were coming, we would have met you by sea and by land. At each stage of your journey to Rome, we would have given you a greater greeting."

"My good lord," Octavia said. "I was not forced to come to Rome so quietly. I did it of my own free will. My lord, Mark Antony, hearing that you were preparing for war, acquainted my grieving ear with the news. Whereupon, I begged his permission for me to return to Rome to try to make peace between you two."

"A return that he quickly granted because you are an obstacle between his lust and him," Octavius Caesar said.

"Do not say that, my lord."

"I have eyes spying on him, and news of his affairs come to me on the wind," Caesar said. "Where do you think he is now?"

"My lord, he is in Athens, Greece."

"No, my most wronged sister," Octavius Caesar said. "Cleopatra nodded at him, and he went to her. He has given his empire up to a whore; and they are now levying the Kings of the earth for war. Antony has assembled to fight for them Bocchus, King of Libya; Archelaus, King of Cappadocia; Philadelphos, King of Paphlagonia; the Thracian King, Adallas; King Malchus of Arabia; the King of Pont; Herod of Judea; Mithridates, King of Comagene; Polemon and Amyntas, the Kings of Mede and Lycaonia, with a longer list of those who wield scepters."

"I am very wretched," Octavia said. "I have divided my heart between two friends who afflict each other!"

"You are welcome here," her brother said.

Using the royal plural, he said, "Your letters delayed the break between Antony and me until we perceived both how you were wrongly led and how we were in danger through neglecting to prepare for war.

"Cheer your heart. Do not be troubled by the times, which drive these strong necessities over your happiness. Instead, let things that are fated to happen occur without crying over them. Welcome to Rome; nothing is dearer to me than you are. Antony has abused you beyond what can be thought, and the high gods, to give you justice, make us who love you their agents. Be comforted as best you can; we always welcome you."

"Welcome, lady," Agrippa said.

"Welcome, dear madam," Maecenas said. "Each heart in Rome loves and pities you. Only the adulterous Antony, most unrestrained in his abominations, turns you away and gives his mighty authority to a whore who clamors against us and turns Antony's mighty authority against us."

"Is this true, sir?" Octavia asked her brother.

"It is most certainly true," Octavius Caesar replied. "Sister, welcome. Please, be patient and calm. You are my dear sister!"

Near Mark Antony's camp in Actium, Cleopatra and Enobarbus were speaking.

"I will talk straight with you — don't doubt it," Cleopatra said.

"But why, why, why?"

"You have spoken against my being in these wars, and say it is not fitting."

"Well, is it? Is it?"

Using the royal plural, Cleopatra replied, "The war has been declared against us, so why shouldn't we be there in person?"

"Well, I could reply with this: If we should serve with stallions and mares together, the stallions would be utterly lost; the mares would bear a soldier and a stallion. Both a soldier and a stallion would ride the mare."

"What do you mean?"

"Your presence in the battle necessarily must confuse and distract Antony; your presence would take from his heart, take from his brain, and take from his time what should not then be spared. You will fluster his heart and his head, and he will have to devote time to you. He is already criticized for levity; and it is said in Rome that Photinus, the eunuch Mardian, and your maidens are in charge of managing this war."

"May Rome sink and may the Romans' tongues that speak against us rot!" Cleopatra said, using the royal plural. "We bear the expense of the war, and, as the ruler of my Kingdom, we will appear there just like a man. Don't speak against it. I will not stay behind."

"I won't bring this up again," Enobarbus said. "I have finished. Here comes the Emperor."

Mark Antony and Canidius, a Lieutenant General, entered the room.

Antony said, "Isn't it strange, Canidius, that Octavius Caesar could cross so quickly the Ionian Sea from Tarentum and Brundusium and capture the city of Toryne in Greece?"

He then asked Cleopatra, "Have you heard this news, sweet?"

"Celerity is never more wondered at than by the negligent," she replied.

"This is a good rebuke, and it can remind even the best of men to taunt slackness," Antony said, adding, "Canidius, we will fight Caesar by sea."

"By sea," Cleopatra said. "Of course!"

"Why will my lord do that?" Canidius asked.

"Because Octavius Caesar dares us to do it."

"But my lord has dared Caesar to fight him in single combat," Enobarbus said.

"True, and to wage this battle at Pharsalia, where Julius Caesar fought Pompey the Great," Canidius said, "but these challenges, which do not give Caesar the advantage, he shakes off and ignores. Like Caesar, you should ignore challenges that do not give you an advantage."

Enobarbus said, "Your ships are not well manned; your mariners are mule drivers, reapers of harvests, people who have been quickly gotten together through being drafted. In Caesar's fleet are those who have often fought against Sextus Pompey. Their ships are nimble; yours are heavy. You will suffer no disgrace for refusing to fight Octavius Caesar at sea because you are prepared to fight him on land."

"I will fight him by sea — by sea," Mark Antony replied.

"Most worthy sir," Enobarbus said, "you thereby throw away the excellent military force you have on land. You split up your army, which mostly consists of war-scarred infantry. You leave unused your own renowned military knowledge. You quite forego the way that promises assurance of victory, and from firm security you give yourself over entirely to chance and hazard."

"I'll fight at sea," Antony said.

"I have sixty ships," Cleopatra said. "Caesar has none better."

"Our surplus of ships we will burn," Antony said, "and, with the rest fully manned, from the head of Actium we will beat the approaching Caesar. But if we fail, we then can beat him back by land."

A messenger entered the room.

Mark Antony asked him, "What is your business here?"

The messenger said, "The news is true, my lord; Octavius Caesar has been sighted. Caesar has conquered Toryne."

"Can Caesar be there in person?" Mark Antony asked. "It is impossible; it is strange that his army should be there."

He then said, "Canidius, our nineteen legions you shall hold by land, and our twelve thousand cavalry. We will go to our ship."

To Cleopatra, he said, "Let's leave, my Thetis!"

Thetis was a sea-goddess and the mother of the Greek hero Achilles, who fought and died in the Trojan War.

A soldier entered the room.

Mark Antony asked him, "How are you, worthy soldier?"

"Oh, noble Emperor, do not fight by sea," the soldier said. "Trust not to rotten planks. Do you mistrust this sword and these my wounds? Let the Egyptians and the Phoenicians go swimming in the sea; we are used to conquer while standing on the earth, and fighting foot to foot."

Mark Antony said merely, "Well, well," and then he said, "Let's go!"

Antony, Cleopatra, and Enobarbus departed.

"By Hercules, I think I am in the right," the soldier said.

"Soldier, you are in the right," Canidius said, "but Antony's whole plan of military action is not based on his strengths. Our leader is led by a woman, and we are the servingmen of women."

"You keep by land the legions and the cavalry undivided, don't you?" the soldier asked.

"Marcus Octavius, Marcus Justeius, Publicola, and Caelius will fight at sea, but we keep ourselves whole and undivided by land," Canidius replied.

He added, "This speed of Caesar's shoots him forward beyond belief."

"While he was still in Rome, his military forces went out in such bits and pieces that all spies were fooled."

"Do you know who is Caesar's Lieutenant General?"

"They say, one Taurus."

"I know the man well," Canidius said.

A messenger entered the room and said, "The Emperor is calling for Canidius to come to him."

"The times are pregnant with news and give birth, each minute, to something new."

— 3.8 —

On a plain near Actium on 2 September 31 B.C.E., Octavius Caesar talked with Taurus, his Lieutenant General.

"Taurus!"

"My lord?"

"Strike not by land; keep the land forces whole and undivided. Do not provoke a land battle until the sea battle is completed."

He gave Taurus a scroll and said, "Do not exceed the orders given to you in this scroll. Our fortune lies upon this gamble."

— 3.9 —

On another part of the plain, Mark Antony was talking to Enobarbus.

Antony said, "We are setting our squadrons on the other side of the hill, in sight of Caesar's battle line of ships; from which place we can count the number of his ships, and proceed accordingly."

Later, after the sea battle was nearly over and Octavius Caesar had triumphed over Mark Antony and Cleopatra, Enobarbus mourned.

"Ruined," Enobarbus mourned. "All is ruined — ruined! I can't bear to look any longer! The *Antoniad*, the Egyptian flagship, with all of Egypt's sixty ships, fled and turned the rudder. Seeing it has blighted my eyes."

A soldier named Scarus walked over to Enobarbus and cursed, "Gods and goddesses, the whole assembly of them!"

"What's the matter with you?"

"The greater part of the world has been lost through utter stupidity," Scarus said. "We have kissed away Kingdoms and provinces."

"How does the battle look like now?"

"On our side it looks like the signs of a plague where death is sure to follow. Yonder ribald and debauched nag of Egypt — I hope the much-ridden Cleopatra catches leprosy! — in the midst of the fight at sea, when the two sides appeared equally matched like twins, with no advantage on either side, or perhaps we appeared to be the elder twin and so had a slight advantage, she hoisted her sails and fled as if she were a cow in June that had been bitten by a gadfly."

"I witnessed that," Enobarbus said. "My eyes sickened at the sight, and they could not endure a further view."

"Cleopatra once being sailed into the wind and having put distance between herself and Caesar's ships, the noble ruin of her magic, Mark Antony, clapped on his sea-wings — his sails — and, like a doting duck, leaving the fight at its height, fled after her. I never saw such a shameful action; experience, manhood, and honor have never before so violated themselves."

"Damn! Damn!" Enobarbus said.

Canidius walked over to the two men.

"Our fortune on the sea is out of breath, and sinks most lamentably," Canidius said. "Had our general been what he knew himself to be, the battle would have gone well, but he has given us an example for our own flight, most grossly and blatantly, by his own flight!"

"Are you thinking about fleeing and deserting?" Enobarbus asked. "Why, then, good night to our hopes indeed."

"Mark Antony and Cleopatra have fled toward the Peloponnesus in Greece," Canidius said.

"It is easy to get to," Scarus said, "and there I will await what happens next."

"To Caesar will I surrender my legions and my cavalry," Canidius said. "Six Kings already have surrendered and through their example show me how to yield to Octavius Caesar."

Enobarbus said, "I'll continue to follow the wounded fortunes of Antony, although my reason tells me not to. My reason sits in the wind against me. My scent blows toward it, and it tracks and hunts me. I should go in the opposite direction — away from Mark Antony."

In a room of Cleopatra's palace in Alexandria, Mark Antony, accompanied by some attendants, was mourning the lost sea battle at Actium.

"Listen!" he said. "The land orders me to tread no more upon it — it is ashamed to bear me! Friends, come here. I am so belated in the world — I am like a traveler who has failed to reach shelter before dark — that I have lost my way forever: I have a ship that is laden with gold; take that, divide it; flee, and make your peace with Octavius Caesar."

His attendants replied, "Flee? We won't flee!"

"I myself have fled," Antony said, "and I have instructed cowards to run and show to the enemy the backs of their shoulders. Friends, leave me. I have myself resolved upon a course of action that has no need of you, so be gone."

Was Antony contemplating committing suicide?

He said, "My treasure is in the harbor, take it. Oh, I followed that woman whom I blush to look upon. My very hairs mutiny: My white hairs reprove my brown hairs for rashness, and my brown hairs reprove my white hairs for fear and doting. Friends, be gone. You shall receive letters from me to some friends who will sweep your way for you so that you can make peace with Caesar. Please, do not look sad, nor make replies of reluctance. Take the opportunity that my despair provides for you. Let that be left that leaves itself — abandon me who has already abandoned himself. Go to the seaside immediately. I will give you possession of that ship and treasure. Leave me, please, for a little while, I ask you now. Leave. I, indeed, have lost the right to command you to leave; therefore, I ask you to leave. I'll see you soon."

The attendants left him, and he sat down.

Cleopatra entered the room. With her were her attendants Charmian and Iras, and Mark Antony's friend Eros.

Eros said, "Gentle madam, go to him, comfort him."

"Do, most dear Queen," Iras said.

"Do!" Charmian said. "Why, what else should you do?"

"Let me sit down," Cleopatra said. "Oh, Juno, Queen of the Roman gods!" She sat down.

"No, no, no, no, no," Mark Antony mourned to himself.

"Do you see Cleopatra here, sir?" Eros asked.

"Oh, damn, damn, damn!" Antony said, ignoring Eros.

"Madam!" Charmian said.

"Madam!" Iras said. "Oh, good Empress!"

"Sir, sir —" Eros said.

"Yes, my lord, yes," Antony said.

Normally, Mark Antony would not call Eros 'my lord.' He was so discouraged that he was not even looking at Eros and therefore did not know to whom he was speaking.

Talking to himself, Mark Antony said, "Octavius Caesar at the Battle of Philippi kept his sword in his sheath as if he were a dancer and his sword was only an ornament, while I struck the lean and wrinkled Cassius; and it was I who defeated the mad Brutus. Caesar alone relied on his lieutenants to do the fighting for him, and he acquired no experience in the brave and splendid battalions of soldiers. But now — it does not matter."

Cleopatra said to Charmian and Iras, "Stand by me. I feel faint."

"The Queen, my lord, the Queen," Eros said to Antony.

"Go to him, madam, speak to him," Iras said to Cleopatra. "He is unqualitied with very shame. He has lost the qualities that made him Antony."

"Well then, sustain me," Cleopatra said. "Help me stand up."

She stood up.

"Most noble sir, arise," Eros said. "The Queen approaches. Her head is bowed, and death will seize her, unless you comfort her and by so doing save her life."

"I have offended reputation and honor," Mark Antony said. "I have committed a very ignoble swerving away from nobility and honor."

Eros said, "Sir, the Queen."

Mark Antony stood up and said to Cleopatra, "Oh, where have you led me, Queen of Egypt? See how I convey my shame out of your eyes and into my eyes? Men ought not to cry, but tears are trickling down my cheeks. I cry when I look back on what I have left behind and destroyed with my dishonor."

"Oh, my lord, my lord, forgive my fearful sails and my fearful flight!" Cleopatra said. "I little thought that you would have followed me."

"Queen of Egypt, you knew too well that my heart was tied by the strings to your rudder, and you should tow me after you wherever you might go," Antony said. "You knew that you had full supremacy over my spirit, and that your beck would turn me away from doing even the bidding of the gods."

"Oh, give me pardon!" Cleopatra said.

"Now I must send my humble entreaties to the young man — Octavius Caesar," Mark Antony said. "I must engage in low dodges and shifty dealings of the kind lowly people must employ. I must do this — I who once played as I pleased with half the bulk of the world, making and marring fortunes. You knew how much you were my conqueror; and you knew that my sword, made weak by my infatuation for you, would always obey my infatuation for you."

"Give me pardon, pardon!" Cleopatra said.

"Let fall not a single tear, I say," Antony replied. "One of your tears is worth all that is won and lost. Give me a kiss; a single kiss repays me for what I have lost. We sent Euphronius, our schoolmaster, to Octavius Caesar. Has he come back? Love, I am full of lead — sorrow is heavy on my heart. Bring some wine, within there, and bring some food! Fortune knows that we scorn her most when most she offers us blows."

In Octavius Caesar's camp in Egypt, Caesar was speaking with his friend Dolabella. Caesar's friend Thidias was also present, along with some attendants.

Octavius Caesar ordered, "Let the messenger sent by Mark Antony appear before us."

An attendant left to carry out the order.

Caesar asked, "Dolabella, do you know him?"

"Caesar, the messenger is the schoolmaster to Antony and Cleopatra's children. This is evidence that Antony's feathers have been plucked; otherwise, he would not have sent so poor a feather from off his wing — not so many months ago, Antony had so many Kings following him that he could send a superfluous King as his messenger."

Euphronius, Mark Antony's messenger, entered the room.

"Approach, and speak," Octavius Caesar ordered.

"Such as I am, I come from Mark Antony," Euphronius said. "I was just recently as petty to his ends as is the morning dew on the myrtle leaf to the grand sea."

"I understand," Caesar said. "State your business."

"Mark Antony salutes you, who are the lord of his fortunes, and he requests that he be allowed to live in Egypt. If you will not allow that, he lessens his request, and he asks you to let him live and breathe between the Heavens and Earth as a private citizen in Athens. This is what Mark Antony requests.

"Now for Cleopatra. Cleopatra acknowledges your greatness; she submits herself to your might; and from you she asks that you allow her heirs to wear the crown of the Ptolemies and rule Egypt — she knows that the crown has been forfeited as if it were a stake in a game of dice and that you are the person who will decide who will wear that crown."

"As for Antony, I have no ears to his request," Octavius Caesar said. "I will not grant him what he requests. The Queen shall not fail to have me listen to her and grant her request, provided that she either drives Antony, her entirely disgraced friend, out of Egypt, or take his life there. If Cleopatra does this, I will grant her request. Take this message to both of them."

"May Fortune pursue you!" Euphronius said.

"Take him safely through the troops," Caesar ordered.

Euphronius and some attendants left.

Octavius Caesar said to Thidias, "Separate Antony and Cleopatra, and get Cleopatra on our side. Promise her, in our name, whatever she wants; promise additional benefits to her as needed. Women are not strong even when they have good fortune, and destitution will cause even a vestal virgin to break her vows. Use your cunning, Thidias. Decide how you will be rewarded for doing this, and we will give it to you as if we were obeying a contract."

"Caesar, I go now," Thidias said.

"Observe how Antony is reacting to his misfortune," Octavius Caesar said. "Tell me what you think his every movement tells about his state of mind."

"Caesar, I shall."

In a room of Cleopatra's palace in Alexandria, Egypt, Cleopatra was speaking to Enobarbus. Charmian and Iras were also present.

Cleopatra asked, "What shall we do, Enobarbus?"

"Think, despair, and die."

Using the royal plural, Cleopatra asked, "Is Antony or we at fault for this?"

"Only Antony is at fault because he made his sexual passion the lord of his reason. So what if you fled from that great front of war, whose opposing ranges of ships frightened each other? Why should he follow after you? The itch of his sexual passion should not then have cut short his captainship; at such a point, when half of the world opposed the other half of the world, with him being the sole cause of dispute, it was no less shameful for him than was his loss of the battle to follow after your fleeing flags, and leave his navy gazing after him in dismay."

"Be silent. Be silent," Cleopatra said.

Mark Antony entered the room with Euphronius, the messenger whom he had sent to Octavius Caesar.

"Is that his answer to me?" Antony asked.

"Yes, my lord."

"The Queen shall then be courteously received by him, as long as she will yield us — me — up."

"So he says," Euphronius replied.

"Let Cleopatra know what Caesar says," Antony said.

To Cleopatra, Antony said, "If you send this grizzled head to the boy Caesar, he will fill your wishes to the brim with principalities."

"That head, my lord?" Cleopatra asked.

Mark Antony said to Euphronius, "Go back to Caesar. Tell him that he wears the rose of youth upon him, and from him the world should note something special. His coin, ships, and legions may belong to a coward, and his agents may be as successful if they were serving a child rather than serving Caesar — Caesar is taking credit for the accomplishments of his agents. I dare Caesar therefore to lay aside his gay comparisons and splendid trappings, and answer me, declined as I am in years and fortune, sword against sword, ourselves alone. I'll write my challenge to him to fight me in single combat. Follow me."

Mark Antony and Euphronius left the room.

Enobarbus thought to himself, sarcastically, *Yes, likely enough, Caesar, who commands huge armies, will divest himself of his huge advantages, and allow himself to participate in a public spectacle and fight against a gladiator! I see that men's judgments are part and parcel of their fortunes; I see that external circumstances and fortune draw the inner man after them so that both suffer together. I can't believe that Mark Antony, who has experienced all measures of fortune from great to poor, can dream that Caesar, riding at the top of Fortune's wheel, will fight in single combat Antony, who is riding at the bottom of Fortune's wheel! Caesar, you have subdued Antony's judgment, too.*

An attendant entered the room and announced, "A messenger has come from Octavius Caesar."

"What! He has come with no more ceremony than that?" Cleopatra said. "See, my women! Against the fading rose, they stop their nose although previously they knelt before the rose's bud."

She ordered, "Admit him, sir."

An attendant left to bring in Caesar's messenger.

Enobarbus thought to himself, *My honor and I begin to quarrel. Loyalty that stays faithful to fools makes our faith mere folly, yet he who can endure to follow with allegiance a fallen lord conquers the person who conquered his master and by doing so earns a place in history.*

Thidias, Caesar's messenger, entered the room.

"What is Caesar's will?" Cleopatra asked.

"Hear it in private," Thidias replied.

"No one is here but friends," Cleopatra said. "Say boldly what you have to say."

"Perhaps they are friends to Mark Antony," Thidias said.

Enobarbus said, "Antony needs as many friends, sir, as Caesar has. If he does not have that many, his case is hopeless, and he does not need us to be his friends. If Caesar will allow it, our master will leap to be his friend. As for us, you know, whose Antony is we are, and Antony is Caesar's."

"So be it," Thidias said. "Most renowned Cleopatra, Caesar asks you to not worry about the situation you are in, but to remember that he is Caesar."

Thidias' words were ambiguous. He wanted Cleopatra to remember that Octavius Caesar was capable of generosity. Cleopatra knew that, but she also knew that Caesar was capable of ruthlessness.

"Go on," Cleopatra said. "Caesar is right royal."

Thidias said, "Caesar knows that you embraced Antony not because you loved him, but because you feared him."

"Oh!" Cleopatra said.

"The scars upon your honor, therefore, Caesar pities and regards as blemishes forced upon you and not as blemishes you deserve."

Cleopatra replied, "Caesar is a god, and he knows where the truth lies. My honor was not freely yielded — it was utterly conquered."

Cleopatra's words were ambiguous. She could mean that she gave in to Antony out of fear, or that she fell completely in love with him when he conquered her heart.

Enobarbus, who was not sure which meaning Cleopatra meant, said to himself, "To be sure of the truth of that, I will ask Antony. Sir, sir, you are so leaky, that we must leave you to your sinking, for even those dearest to you quit you."

Thinking of rats leaving a sinking ship, he left the room.

Thidias said, "Shall I tell Caesar what you request from him? He almost begs you to ask him to give you what you want. It would much please him if you were to make a staff of his fortunes that you would lean upon, but it would warm his spirits to hear from me that you had left Antony, and put yourself under the protection of Caesar, who is the universal landlord — he now rules the world."

"What's your name?" Cleopatra asked.

"My name is Thidias."

"Most kind messenger, say to great Caesar this: With you as my deputy, I kiss his conquering hand. Tell him that I am prompt to lay my crown at his feet, and at his feet to kneel. Tell him that from his breath — that all must obey — I will hear the sentence that he gives to me, the Queen of Egypt."

"This is your noblest course," Thidias said. "When a wise person meets with bad fortune, if the wise person accepts the bad fortune, nothing can shake the person's wisdom — it is wise to accept what must occur. Give me permission to lay my lips on your hand and kiss it."

Cleopatra offered him her hand and said, "Julius Caesar, the father of Octavius Caesar, often, when he was thinking about conquering Kingdoms, bestowed his lips on that unworthy place, as if it rained kisses."

Thidias kissed Cleopatra's hand just as Mark Antony and Enobarbus entered the room.

Seeing the kiss, Antony was immediately angry.

Seeing the kiss, Enobarbus thought, *This messenger will be whipped. A mere messenger ought not to kiss the hand of a Queen.*

"You are giving favors to lackeys, by Jove who thunders!" Antony said to Cleopatra.

He said contemptuously to Thidias, "Who are you, fellow?"

"One who obeys the orders of the greatest man, and the worthiest to have his commands obeyed."

Mark Antony called for attendants: "Come here!"

He then said, "Ah, you kite!"

A kite is a hawk that feeds on disgusting things. Was Antony insulting Cleopatra for allowing a lackey to kiss her hand? Or was he insulting Thidias for using a position of power to make Cleopatra allow him to kiss her hand?

The attendants were slow in responding to Antony's call.

Antony cursed, "Gods and devils! Authority now melts from me. Just recently, I would cry 'Ho!' and Kings would start forth like boys scrambling to pick up desired trinkets strewn on the ground before them and they would ask me, 'What is your will?'"

He called to his attendants, "Have you no ears? I am still Antony."

Some attendants entered the room, and Antony ordered, "Take away from here this rascal, and whip him."

Enobarbus thought, *It is better to play with a lion's cub than with an old lion that is dying.*

Mark Antony cursed, "Moon and stars! Whip him. I would order the same even if I were to find twenty of the greatest tribute-paying rulers who acknowledge Caesar so saucy with the hand of this woman here — what's her name? What is the name of this woman who used to be Cleopatra? Whip him, fellows, until, like a boy, you see him cringe his face in pain, and whine aloud for mercy. Take him away from here."

"Mark Antony!" Thidias said.

He may have wanted Antony to know that as a messenger of Octavius Caesar, he was under the protection of Caesar and so whipping him would be a direct insult to Caesar.

"Tug him away," Antony said. "Once he has been whipped, bring him here again. This rascal of Caesar's shall run an errand and take a message from us to him."

The attendants took Thidias away.

Mark Antony said to Cleopatra, "You were half blighted before I knew you! Have I left my pillow unused in Rome, forgone the begetting of legitimate children by Octavia, a gem of women, just so I can be abused by a woman who looks favorably on servants such as this messenger from Caesar?"

"My good lord —" Cleopatra began.

"You have always been a boggler," Antony said.

In falconry, a boggler is a falcon that does not chase just one bird, but instead chases one and then another and then another.

He continued, "But when we become hardened to our depravity — a misery! — the wise gods sew shut and blind our eyes. The gods make our clear judgments drop in our own filth. The gods make us adore our errors. The gods laugh at us while we strut to our destruction."

"Has it come to this?" Cleopatra asked.

"I found you as a cold crumb on dead Julius Caesar's platter. You were a leftover of Gnaeus Pompey's. In addition, you have enjoyed hotter lecherous hours that have not been gossiped about. I am sure that although you can guess what temperance should be, you have not experienced it."

"Why are you saying these things?" Cleopatra asked.

"You have let a fellow who will take a tip and say, 'May God reward you!' be familiar with my playfellow, your hand — which has signed Kingly documents and sealed the pledges of noble lovers!" Mark Antony said. "Oh, if I were upon the hill of Basan, I would outroar the horned herd!"

Herds of horned bulls were on the hill of Basan. Horns are the symbol of a cuckold, and so Antony was saying that because of the actions of Cleopatra, he would be the biggest and loudest cuckold in that horned herd.

He continued, "I have savage cause to bellow, and to protest in a civilized manner would be like a neck with a noose around it thanking the hangman for being efficient in doing his job."

The attendants returned with Thidias.

"Has he been whipped?" Mark Antony asked.

"Soundly, my lord," the first attendant replied.

"Did he cry? Did he ask for mercy?"

"He did ask for mercy," the first attendant replied.

Mark Antony said to Thidias, "If your father is still alive, let him regret that you were not born his daughter, and as for you, be sorry to follow Caesar in his triumphal procession, since you have been whipped for following him. And henceforth may seeing the white hand of a lady give you a fever and make you shiver when you look at it. Go back to Octavius Caesar and tell him about your treatment here. Be sure that you say that he makes me angry with him; for he seems proud and disdainful, harping on what I am and not what he knew I was. He makes me angry, and at this time it is very easy to do it, now that my good stars, which were my former guides, have left their orbits and shot their fires into the abyss of Hell. If Caesar dislikes my speech and what has been done to you, tell him that he has Hipparchus, my freed slave, whom he may at his pleasure whip, or hang, or torture, as he shall like, to pay me back. Tell him these things. Leave and take with you your stripes — go!"

Thidias left.

"Have you finished yet?" Cleopatra asked Mark Antony.

Antony said, "Alas, our Earthly moon — Cleopatra — is now eclipsed; and it portends the fall of Antony!"

Cleopatra, an Earthly Queen, was often associated with the Moon goddess Isis. In this society, an eclipse of the Moon was thought to be a portent of imminent disaster.

"I must wait until he is finished," Cleopatra said.

"To flatter Caesar, would you mingle eyes and flirt with a servant who helps him get dressed?" Antony asked.

"Don't you know me yet?" Cleopatra asked.

"Are you cold-hearted toward me?"

"Ah, dear, if I am, from my cold heart let Heaven engender hail, and poison it in the source; and let the first stone drop on my neck. As the poisoned hailstone melts, so let it dissolve my life! Let the next hailstone smite my son Caesarion! By degrees let the hailstones kill all the children who have come from my womb and kill all my brave Egyptians. Let the melting of the hailstones from this storm kill them all, and let them lie without graves until the flies and gnats of the Nile River eat them and so give them burial!"

"I am satisfied," Mark Antony said. He ceased to be jealous of and angry at Cleopatra.

He added, "Octavius Caesar has made his camp at and is besieging Alexandria, where I will oppose his fate and destiny. Our army by land has nobly held together; our divided navy has knit together again, and it sails — it is as threatening as the sea. Where have you been, my heart? Do you hear me, lady? If from the battlefield I shall return once more to kiss these lips of yours, I will appear bloody and full of vigor; my sword and I will earn our place in history. There's hope in battle yet."

"That's my brave lord!"

"I will be treble-sinewed, -hearted, and -breathed — I will have the strength, courage, and endurance of three men — and I will fight ferociously. When my fortune was prosperous and happy, I allowed men to ransom their lives for jests and trifles, but now I'll set my teeth, and send to darkness and Hell all who oppose me. Come, let's have one more festive night. Call to me all my sad and serious captains; fill our bowls with wine once more; let's mock the midnight bell."

"It is my birthday," Cleopatra said. "I had thought to have observed it poorly, but since my lord is Antony again, I will be Cleopatra. We will be festive."

"We will yet do well."

Cleopatra ordered, "Call all of Antony's noble captains to my lord."

Mark Antony said, "Do so. We'll speak to them. Tonight I'll force the wine to peep through their scars — their white scars will appear to be red from the wine they have drunk. Come on, my Queen; there's sap — life — in it yet. The next time I fight, I'll make Death love me. I will compete with Death's pestilential scythe and kill as many as the plague kills."

Everyone left except for Enobarbus, who said to himself, "Now Antony will outstare the lightning. To be furious is to be frightened out of fear. He is so angry that he is unable to feel fear, and in that mood a dove will peck a hawk. I have always seen that a diminution in our captain's brain restores his heart. When his reason grows weaker, his bravery grows stronger. But when valor preys on reason, it eats the sword it fights with. Courage in battle requires a good brain if it is to be effective. I will seek some way to leave Antony and stop serving him."

CHAPTER 4

— 4.1 —

In Octavius Caesar's camp before Alexandria, Egypt, Caesar was discussing with his friends Maecenas and Agrippa the message that Thidias had brought from Mark Antony.

Caesar said, "He calls me 'boy,' and he chides me as if he had the power to beat me out of Egypt. He has whipped my messenger with rods. He dares me to personal combat: Caesar against Antony. Let the old ruffian know I have many other ways to die; in the meantime, I laugh at his challenge."

"Caesar must think," Maecenas said, "that when one so great begins to rage, he's hunted to exhaustion, even to falling. Give him no time to breathe, but now take advantage of his distracting anger. Never has anger protected angry people well."

"Let our top commanders know that tomorrow we intend to fight the last of many battles," Caesar said. "Within our ranks of soldiers we have enough of those who served Mark Antony just recently to capture him. See that this is done, and give the army a feast. We have enough provisions to do it, and they have earned the expense. Poor Antony!"

In a room of Cleopatra's palace at Alexandria, Mark Antony, Cleopatra, Domitius Enobarbus, Charmian, Iras, Alexas, and others were assembled.

"Caesar will not fight with me, Domitius," Mark Antony said.

"No, he won't."

"Why won't he fight with me?"

"He thinks, since his fortunes are twenty times better than yours, his army against yours is twenty men to one," Enobarbus replied.

"Tomorrow, soldier, by sea and land I'll fight," Mark Antony said. "Either I will live, or by bathing my dying honor in blood I will make my honor live again. Will you fight well?"

"I'll strike, and cry, 'Take all.'"

Enobarbus' words were ambiguous. They could mean that he would strike fiercely at the enemy in battle, or that he would strike sail and surrender. The words "Take all" were those of a desperate gambler betting all he had left.

"Well said," Mark Antony replied. "Come on. Call forth my household servants. Let's feast tonight and be bounteous at our meal."

A few male servants entered the room and Antony said to them, "Give me your hand. You have been truly honest ... so have you ... you ... and you ... and you ... you have served me well, and Kings have also served me."

Cleopatra asked Enobarbus quietly, "What is Antony doing?"

Enobarbus quietly replied, "He has one of those odd moods that sorrow shoots out of the mind."

Antony continued speaking to the servants: "And you are honest, too. I wish I could be made as many men as you are, and all of you were rolled up together in one Antony, so that I could do you service as good as you have done for me."

The servants were horrified: "The gods forbid!"

"Well, my good fellows," Antony said, "wait on me tonight. Do not scant when filling my cup with wine, and make as much of me as when my empire was your fellow — my servant — and obeyed my commands."

"What does he mean?" Cleopatra quietly asked Enobarbus.

"He means to make his followers weep," he quietly replied.

"Serve me tonight," Antony said. "Maybe it is the end of your duty to me. Perhaps you shall not see me any more; or if you do, you will see a mangled ghost. Perhaps tomorrow you'll serve another master. I look on you as one who takes his leave of you. My honest friends, I am not firing you and turning you away, but like a master who is married to your good service, I stay with you until death. Serve me tonight for two hours — I ask no more, and may the gods reward you for it!"

"What do you mean, sir, by giving your servants this discomfort?" Enobarbus said to Antony. "Look, they are crying, and I, an ass, am onion-eyed — tears are trickling from my eyes. For shame! Do not transform us into women."

Mark Antony said, "May a witch enchant me if I meant to turn all of you into women! May grace grow where those teardrops fall! My hearty friends, you take me in too melancholy a sense — I spoke to you to comfort you. I want you to burn this night with torches and make it brilliant. Know, my hearts, I have high hope for tomorrow; and I will lead you where I expect to find victorious life instead of an honorable death. Let's go to supper. Come, and we will drown our serious thoughts with wine."

In Alexandria, in front of Cleopatra's palace, Mark Antony's soldiers were preparing for guard duty.

Two soldiers arrived.

The first soldier said, "Brother, good night. Tomorrow is the day of the battle."

"It will bring matters to an end, one way or the other," the second soldier said. "Fare you well. Heard you about anything strange in the streets?"

"Nothing. What is the news?"

"Probably it is only a rumor. Good night to you."

"Well, sir, good night," the first soldier said.

Two more soldiers arrived.

The second soldier said to them, "Soldiers, have an attentive watch."

"You, too," the third soldier said. "Good night."

The two groups of soldiers moved away from each other and started their guard duty.

The second soldier said, "Here we are, in the correct positions for guard duty. If our navy thrives tomorrow, I have an absolute hope that our army will stand up on land and be victorious."

"It is a brave army," the first soldier said, "and very resolute."

The sound of oboes came from underground.

"Silence!" the second soldier said. "What is that noise?"

The first soldier said, "Listen! Listen!"

"Hark!" the second soldier said.

"Music is in the air," the first soldier said.

At the other guard post, the third soldier said, "It is coming from under the ground."

"This is a good sign, isn't it?" the fourth soldier said.

"No," the third soldier replied.

At the first guard post, the first soldier said to the second soldier, "Quiet, I say! What does this mean?"

The second soldier said, "It means that the god Hercules, whom Antony loved, is now leaving him."

"Let's walk and see if the other guards hear what we do," the first soldier said.

They walked to the second guard post, and the second soldier asked, "How are you, sirs?"

They all began to speak at the same time: "How are you! How are you? Do you hear this music?"

The first soldier said, "Yes, I hear the music. Isn't it strange?"

"Do you hear the music, sirs? Do you hear it?" the third soldier asked.

"Let's follow the noise as far as we can and still keep our guard," the first soldier said. "Let's see how the music finishes."

"Agreed," the other soldiers said. "This music is strange."

In a room of Cleopatra's palace were Mark Antony and Cleopatra. Attending them were Charmian and others.

Mark Antony called, "Bring me my armor, Eros!"

"Sleep a little," Cleopatra said.

"No, my darling," Antony replied.

He called again, "Eros, come here! Bring me my armor, Eros!"

Eros arrived, carrying Antony's armor.

"Come good fellow, put my iron armor on me," Mark Antony said to Eros. "If good fortune is not ours today, it is because we will deny her. Come on."

"I'll help, too," Cleopatra said. She picked up a piece of armor and asked, "What's this for? Where does it go?"

"Ah, let it be, let it alone!" Antony said. "You are the armorer of my heart — you give me courage."

Cleopatra tried to put a piece of armor on Mark Antony, but he told her, "That is the wrong way. It goes like this."

She replied, "I'll help. Yes, indeed, it must go like this."

"That's right," Antony said. "We shall thrive now."

He said to Eros, "Do you see how Cleopatra is helping me, my good fellow? Go and put on your armor."

"In a little while, sir," Eros replied.

"Is not this buckled well?" Cleopatra said, referring to a piece of Antony's armor.

"It is very excellently done," Antony replied. "He who unbuckles this before I am pleased to take it off and rest shall hear a storm of blows against his armor."

Both Eros and Cleopatra continued to help put on Antony's armor.

Antony said, "You are fumbling, Eros. My Queen is a squire and armor-bearer who is more skilled at this than you are. Hurry."

He said to Cleopatra, "Oh, love, I wish that you could see me in the battle today. If you could, you would see and know war — the royal occupation! You would see a true craftsman at work in the battle!"

A soldier wearing armor entered the room, and Mark Antony said to him, "Good morning to you, and welcome. You look like a man who knows a warlike charge. We rise early to go to the business that we love, and we go to it with delight."

The soldier replied, "A thousand soldiers, sir, early though it is, have put on their riveted armor, and they are waiting for you at the gate."

The shouts of soldiers and the sound of trumpets came from outside the palace.

Some captains and soldiers entered the room.

"The morning is fair," a captain said. "Good morning, general."

All said, "Good morning, general."

"The trumpet was well blown, lads," Antony said. "This morning, like the spirit of a youth who intends to do something noteworthy in his life, begins early."

He said to Cleopatra, who was still helping him put on his armor, "So. Come. Give me that. It goes this way; well done. May you fare well, dame, whatever becomes of me. This is a soldier's kiss."

He kissed Cleopatra and then said, "I would deserve shameful rebuke and reproach if I were to insist on a formal leave-taking. I'll leave you now, like a man of steel."

He said to his captains and soldiers, "You who will fight, follow me closely. I'll take you to the battle," and then he said to Cleopatra, "*Adieu.*"

Mark Antony, Eros, and the captains and soldiers exited.

"Please, retire to your chamber," Charmian said to Cleopatra.

"Lead me there," Cleopatra said. "Mark Antony goes forth gallantly. I wish that Octavius Caesar and he could determine the outcome of this great war in single combat! Then Antony ... but now ... well, let's go."

In Mark Antony's camp at Alexandria, a soldier met Antony and Eros. This soldier had advised Antony to fight a land battle and not a sea battle at Actium.

The soldier said, "May the gods make this a happy day for Antony!"

"I wish that you and those scars of yours had earlier prevailed to make me fight on land!" Antony replied.

"If you had done so, the Kings who have revolted against you, and the soldier who has this morning left you, would still be following at your heels."

"Who has left me this morning?"

"Who!" the soldier said, surprised that Antony did not already know. "One always close to you. If you call for Enobarbus, he shall not hear you; or if he does, from Caesar's camp he will say, 'I am not one of your soldiers.'"

"What are you saying?" Mark Antony asked.

"Sir, Enobarbus deserted. He is with Caesar."

Eros said, "Sir, Enobarbus left behind his chests and treasure."

"Is he gone?" Antony asked.

"Most certainly," the soldier replied.

"Go, Eros, and send his treasure after him," Antony ordered. "Do it. Detain no jot, I order you. Write to him — I will sign the letter — and give him gentle *adieus* and greetings. Say that I hope that he never finds another reason to change his master. Oh, my bad fortune has corrupted honest men! Hurry. Oh, Enobarbus!"

At Octavius Caesar's camp at Alexandria were Caesar, Agrippa, Enobarbus, and others.

Caesar said, "Go forth, Agrippa, and begin the battle. Our will is that Antony be taken alive. Make sure that everyone knows that."

"Caesar, I shall."

He departed to carry out the order.

Octavius Caesar said, "The time of universal peace is near. If this proves to be a prosperous day, the three corners of the world — Europe, Asia, and Africa — shall bear the olive freely and enjoy peace."

A messenger arrived and said, "Antony has come onto the battlefield."

Caesar said, "Go order Agrippa to place those who have revolted against and deserted Antony in the front lines, so that Antony may seem to spend his fury upon himself and his own forces."

Everyone exited except Enobarbus, who said to himself, "Alexas revolted against Mark Antony, and he went to Judea seemingly to carry out Antony's orders. In Judea, Alexas persuaded great Herod to support Caesar and cease to support Antony. In return for Alexas' pains, Caesar has hanged him. Canidius and the rest who fell away from Mark Antony have employment, but no positions of honorable trust. I have done something evil, for which I accuse myself so sorely that I will never be happy again."

A soldier of Caesar's walked up to him and said, "Enobarbus, Antony has sent all your treasure to you, along with a gift. Antony's messenger came while I was on guard duty, and he is now unloading his mules at your tent."

"I give my treasure to you," Enobarbus said.

"Stop joking, Enobarbus," the soldier replied. "I am telling you the truth. It is best that you escort the bringer of your treasure safely out of the camp. I must attend to my duty, or I would do it myself. Your Emperor continues to act generously, like a Jove."

The soldier left.

"I am the worst villain on the earth," Enobarbus said to himself, "and I feel it the most. Oh, Antony, you fount of generosity, how well would you have paid me for good service, when you crown my depravity and wickedness with gold! This explodes my heart. If swift thought does not break my heart, a swifter means of breaking it shall out-strike my thought and do more damage, but guilty thoughts will break my heart, I feel. Will I fight against you? No! I will go and find some ditch in which I can die; the foulest ditch and fate best suit the latter part of my life."

On the battlefield, Agrippa said to some of Octavius Caesar's soldiers, "Retreat, we have advanced too far. Caesar himself is hard pressed, and the forces against us exceed what we expected."

In another part of the battlefield, Mark Antony and a wounded soldier named Scarus talked.

"Oh, my brave Emperor," Scarus said, "this battle is well fought indeed! Had we fought like this in our earlier battle, we would have driven them home with blows and bandages on their heads."

"You are bleeding a lot," Mark Antony said.

"I had a wound here that was like a T," Scarus said, pointing to the wound, "but now it has been made into an H." He pronounced "H" like "aitch," which sounded similar to "ache." Even wounded, he was able to joke.

"The enemy soldiers are retreating," Antony said.

"We'll beat them so badly that they will hide in latrines," Scarus said. "I still have room for six more wounds."

Eros came over to them and said to Antony, "They are beaten, sir, and our superiority shows that we have won a clear victory over them."

"Let us wound their backs, and snatch them up, as we take hares, from behind," Scarus said. "It is good entertainment to maul a fleeing enemy soldier."

"I will reward you once for your good humor, and ten-fold for your good bravery," Antony replied to Scarus. "Come with me."

Scarus replied, "I'll limp and follow you."

Later, Mark Antony, Scarus, and others stood under the walls of Alexandria.

Antony said, "We have beaten Octavius Caesar back to his camp. Let someone run ahead of us and let Queen Cleopatra know of our deeds in battle."

An attendant departed to carry out the order.

Antony continued, "Tomorrow, before the Sun dawns and sees us, we'll spill the blood that has today escaped from us. I thank you all because all of you are valiant in battle, and you have fought not as if you served my cause, but as if my cause had been your own cause. All of you have fought like the great Trojan War hero Hector."

Hector was the greatest Trojan warrior, but he died in combat and the Trojans lost the war.

Antony continued, "Enter the city, embrace your wives and your friends, and tell them your feats in battle today while they with joyful tears wash the congealed blood from your wounds, and kiss the honored gashes and make them whole."

He said to Scarus, "Give me your hand."

They shook hands.

Cleopatra arrived with her attendants.

Antony said to Scarus, "To this great enchantress I'll commend your acts and have her thank and bless you."

Antony said to Cleopatra, "Oh, you light of the world, hug my armored neck as if you were a necklace. Leap with all your fine clothing through my armor that has withstood the enemy and enter my heart and enjoy this triumph in my panting breast."

"Lord of lords!" Cleopatra said. "Oh, infinite virtue, have you come smiling uncaught from the world's great snare? Have you really survived this great battle?"

"My nightingale, we have beaten them to their beds," Antony replied.

Using the royal plural, he said, "What, girl! Although grey hairs somewhat mingle with our younger brown hairs, yet we have a brain that nourishes our nerves, sinews, and muscles and we can compete with younger men and match them goal for goal."

Pointing to Scarus, Antony said, "Behold this man. Commend to his lips your hand and show him your favor."

Cleopatra held her hand out to Scarus.

"Kiss it, my warrior," Antony said.

Scarus kissed her hand.

Antony said to Cleopatra, "He has fought today as if he were a god who hated Mankind and actively sought to destroy it."

"I'll give you, friend," Cleopatra said to Scarus, "a suit of armor made of gold; it belonged to a King."

"He has deserved it, and he would deserve it even if it were decorated with valuable jewels like the chariot of the Sun-god: Phoebus Apollo," Antony said.

He shook hands again with Scarus and said to his soldiers, "Through Alexandria make a jolly march. Let us carry our hacked shields with pride, such as becomes the men who own them. If our great palace had the capacity to hold all this host of soldiers, we all would eat together, and drink toasts to the next day's fate, which promises royal peril and the greatest danger. Trumpeters, with a brazen din blast the city's ears; mingle your sound with that of rattling drums. Let the noise echo from the sky so that Heaven and Earth may strike their sounds together, applauding our entry into Alexandria."

Some sentinels stood at the guard post in Octavius Caesar's camp outside Alexandria.

The first soldier said, "If we are not relieved within this hour, we must return to the guardhouse. The night is bright and shiny with moonlight, and they say we shall begin getting ready for battle by the second hour of the morning."

"Yesterday's battle was cruel to us," the second soldier said.

Enobarbus came near the soldiers, but he did not see them.

Thinking that he was alone, he said to himself, "Oh, bear witness, night —"

"Who is this man?" the third soldier asked quietly.

"Stay hidden, and listen to him," the second soldier replied.

"Be witness to me, oh, you blessed Moon," Enobarbus said. "When men who revolt against their masters are recorded with disgrace in the history books, remember that poor Enobarbus repented his disgraceful actions before your face!"

"Enobarbus!" the first soldier said.

"Quiet!" the third soldier said.

Enobarbus continued, "Oh, sovereign mistress of true melancholy, discharge upon me the poisonous damp of night as if you were wringing out a sponge."

In this society, people believed that breathing night air was unhealthy.

"I wish that my life, which is a complete rebel to my will that prefers that I be dead, may hang no longer on me. Throw my heart against the hard flintiness of my sin. Let my heart dry out with grief and break up into powder, and finish all my foul thoughts. Antony, you are nobler than my revolt against you is infamous. May you personally forgive me, but let the world remember me in its records as a master-leaver and a fugitive. Oh, Antony! Oh, Antony!"

Enobarbus died from excessive grief.

The second soldier said, "Let's speak to him."

"Let's listen to him," the first soldier said, "because the things he says may concern Caesar."

"Let's do so," the third soldier said. "But he is sleeping."

"No, he has fainted," the first soldier said. "So bad a prayer as his has never been a prelude to sleep."

"Let's go to him," the second soldier said.

They went to him, and the third soldier said, "Wake up, sir, wake up; speak to us."

The second soldier said, "Do you hear us, sir?"

"The hand of death has caught him," the first soldier said.

Drums quietly sounded.

"Listen!" the first soldier said. "The drums quietly wake up the sleepers. Let us carry him to the guardhouse. He is an important person. Our guard duty has ended."

The third soldier said, "Come on, then. He may yet recover."

They carried away the corpse of Enobarbus.

Mark Antony said to Scarus, "Octavius Caesar is preparing today for a sea battle. He does not want to fight us on land."

"He does not want to fight us by land or sea," Scarus said. "We are prepared to fight him in both kinds of battles."

"I wish that they would fight in the fire or in the air," Antony said. "We would fight there, too. But these are my orders. Our infantry shall stay with us upon the hills next to the city. I have given orders for a sea battle. Our ships have left the harbor. From here, we can best see their position and watch the battle."

— 4.11 —

Octavius Caesar said to his soldiers, "Unless we are attacked, we will not fight on land. I don't think that we will be attacked because Antony is using his best soldiers to man his galleys. Let's go to the valleys, and hold the best positions we can."

— 4.12 —

Mark Antony said to Scarus, "The ships are still not joined in battle. Where that pine tree stands yonder, I will go and see what is happening. I'll bring you word soon of how the battle is likely to go."

He walked to the pine tree.

Scarus said to himself, "Swallows have built their nests in Cleopatra's ships. The augurs say that they do not know and cannot tell what this means, but they look grim and dare not say what they know. Antony is valiant, and he is dejected; and, by turns, his varying fortunes give him hope, and then they give him fear, about what he has and what he has not."

Sounds of many ships at sea were heard, and soon Mark Antony returned and said, "All is lost; this foul Egyptian — Cleopatra — has betrayed me. My fleet has surrendered to the foe, and yonder they cast their caps up high in the air and drink together like long-lost friends. Cleopatra is a triple-turned whore! She turned from Gnaeus Pompey to Julius Caesar, from Julius Caesar to me, and from me to Octavius Caesar! Cleopatra has sold me to this novice named Octavius Caesar, and my heart makes wars only on her."

He ordered Scarus, "Order all my soldiers to flee. For when I am revenged upon Cleopatra, my enchantress, I have done all that I will do in this life. Order them all to flee — go!"

Scarus left.

Antony said to himself, "Oh, Sun, your dawn I shall see no more. Good fortune and Antony part here; even now do we shake hands in parting. Has all come to this? The soldiers who followed me at my heels like a cocker spaniel, to whom I gave what they wished, now melt away from me and give their loyalty to blossoming Caesar. I am like a pine tree that has been stripped of its bark, although I overtopped everyone else. I have been betrayed! Oh, this false soul of Egypt! This grave enchantress — her eye summoned forth my wars, and called them home; her bosom was my crown, my chief desire in life — like a typical Egyptian whore, has, as if she were playing a game with the intention of cheating me, beguiled me and caused me total defeat."

Antony called, "Eros! Where are you, Eros?"

Cleopatra walked over to Mark Antony.

Seeing her, he said, "You enchantress! Avaunt! Get away from me!"

"Why is my lord enraged against his love?" Cleopatra asked.

"Vanish, or I shall give you what you deserve, and thereby blemish Caesar's triumph," Antony said.

He meant that he was tempted to kill Cleopatra. It would give him a feeling of revenge, and it would also diminish the triumphal procession that Octavius Caesar would hold in Rome because Caesar would like to capture Cleopatra so that he could exhibit her to the Romans in his triumphal procession.

Antony said to Cleopatra, "Let Caesar capture you, and hoist you up to the shouting Roman commoners. You will walk behind his chariot, like the greatest stain of all your sex; most monster-like, you will be shown to the poorest of the poor diminutives, to idiots and cretins; and patient Octavia will rake your face up and down with her long and sharp fingernails."

Cleopatra exited.

"It is well you have gone," Antony said to himself, "if it is well to live, but it would be better if you died as a result of my fury because one death now might prevent many more. If you die now, your life is ended. But if you stay alive now, you will worry about being killed later and you will suffer many deaths in your imagination."

Antony called, "Eros!"

He said to himself, "The shirt of Nessus is upon me. Teach me your rage, Alcides, you who are my ancestor and are better known as Hercules. Let me lodge Lichas on the horns of the Moon, and with those hands that grasped the heaviest club, subdue my worthiest self."

Antony was thinking of emulating the death of club-wielding Hercules, strongman of the ancient world. A Centaur named Nessus had attempted to rape Hercules' wife, Deianira, so Hercules had shot him with an arrow and killed him. Nessus told Deianira to take his shirt, which was stained with his blood, and keep it because if Hercules ever ceased to love her, the shirt would cast a magical spell over him and make him love her again. Eventually, Deianira thought that Hercules had fallen out of love with her, so she gave Hercules' servant Lichas Nessus' bloodstained shirt to take to Hercules, but when Hercules put on the shirt, Nessus' blood burned him and melted his flesh, causing him agonizing pain. He was in so much pain that he grabbed Lichas and hurled him high into the air — Lichas fell into the sea. Hercules then committed suicide by climbing onto a funeral pyre and setting it on fire.

Antony said about Cleopatra, "The witch shall die. To the young Roman boy — Octavius Caesar — she has sold me, and I have been utterly defeated because of her plot — she dies for it."

He called again, "Eros!"

— 4.13 —

In her palace in Alexandria, Cleopatra worried about what Mark Antony might do to her. With her were Charmian, Iras, and Mardian.

"Help me, my women!" Cleopatra said. "Oh, Antony is more mad than Great Ajax, son of Telamon, was for his shield; the boar of Thessaly was never so foaming at the mouth."

After Achilles died in the Trojan War, the Greeks decided to award his armor, including his shield, which had been created by the blacksmith god, Vulcan, to a great Greek warrior. The two contestants for the armor were Great Ajax and Ulysses. The armor was awarded to Ulysses, and Great Ajax became insane as a result. He tortured sheep, thinking that they were Ulysses and Agamemnon, the leader of the Greeks in the Trojan War. After regaining his sanity, Great Ajax committed suicide.

The goddess Diana once sent a huge boar to ravage Thessaly because the people of Thessaly had neglected to sacrifice to her.

Charmian advised Cleopatra, "Go to the monument that will be your tomb after you die! There lock yourself, and send Antony word that you are dead. The soul and body tear not more in parting than the departure of greatness."

Losing one's greatness is as painful as the separation of soul from body at the time of death. Mark Antony was in pain because he had lost his greatness.

Cleopatra said, "Let's go to the monument! Mardian, go and tell Antony that I have slain myself. Tell him that the last word I spoke was 'Antony,' and when you tell this tale, please make him feel pity for me. Go, Mardian, and tell me how he takes the news of my death. To the monument!"

Mark Antony and Eros spoke together in a room of Cleopatra's palace.

Antony asked, "Eros, can you still see me?"

Antony was so discouraged by the loss of his greatness that he worried about being so diminished that he could not be seen.

"Yes, noble lord."

"Sometimes we see a cloud that looks like a dragon," Antony said. "A cloud sometimes looks like a bear or lion, a towering citadel, an overhanging rock, a mountain with two peaks, or a blue promontory with trees upon it that nod to the world and fool our eyes with air. You have seen such signs; they are the sights that we see in the twilight of the evening."

"Yes, my lord."

"We see that which appears now to be a horse, but as quickly as thought the cloud disperses and makes the image indistinct, as water is when it enters a larger mass of water."

"That is true, my lord."

"My good servant Eros, your captain is now such a body of cloud. I am Antony now, but I cannot hold this visible shape, my lad. I made these wars for the Queen of Egypt — whose heart I thought I had, for she had mine; while my heart belonged to me, it had joined to it the hearts of a million followers, who are now lost. Eros, Cleopatra has stacked the deck in favor of Octavius Caesar, and she has played the cards in such a way as to allow him to trump my high card and triumph over me."

Using the royal plural, Antony added, "No, do not weep, gentle Eros; there is something left to us — we ourselves can end ourselves. I can commit suicide."

Mardian the eunuch arrived, bearing Cleopatra's message.

Seeing him, Antony said, "Your vile lady has robbed me of my sword and my masculinity!"

"No, Antony," Mardian said. "My mistress loved you, and her fortunes were mingled entirely with yours. She did not betray you."

"Go away from here, saucy eunuch; shut up!" Antony said. "She has betrayed me, and she shall die the death of a traitor."

"The death of one person can be paid only once," Mardian said, "and that is a debt that she has already paid. What you want to do has already been done for you. The last words she spoke were 'Antony! Most noble Antony!' In the midst of a tearing groan, the name of Antony broke in two. She spoke part of your name and died without speaking the other part. She gave up her life, but your name is buried in her."

"Is she dead, then?" Mark Antony asked.

"Yes, she is dead."

"Take my armor off me, Eros," Antony ordered. "The long day's task is done, and we must sleep."

He said to Mardian, "Your being allowed to leave here safely pays you richly for your labor. Such a message deserves much worse. Go."

Mardian exited.

Antony ordered Eros, "Take my armor off, pluck it off me."

He added, "Great Ajax's shield with its seven layers of leather cannot keep this battery of blows from my heart. Oh, split apart, my sides! Heart, for once be stronger than your container — crack the frail body that holds you!

"Hurry, Eros, hurry! I am no longer a soldier. Battered pieces of armor, leave me. You have been nobly borne."

He ordered Eros, "Leave me and let me alone for a while."

Eros exited.

Antony said to himself, "I will come after you and overtake you, Cleopatra, and weep for you to pardon me. So it must be, because now all further life is torture. Since the torch of my love and my life is out, I will lie down and stray no farther. Now all labor mars what it does. Yes, it is as if I were in a trap in which the more I struggle the more firmly I am trapped. Let me finish my life and seal it, and all is finished."

Antony called, "Eros!"

He said to himself, "I am coming to you, my Queen."

He called again, "Eros!"

He said to himself, "Wait for me, Cleopatra. In the Heavenly fields where souls lie on flowers, we'll go hand in hand, and with our lively conduct we will make the ghosts gaze at us. Dido and her Aeneas shall lack followers, and all the field will be ours."

Aeneas had had an affair with Dido, the Queen of Carthage, a great city in Africa, but Aeneas had obeyed the will of the gods and deserted Dido in order to go to Italy and fulfill his destiny of becoming an important ancestor of the Romans. While he was still alive, Aeneas had visited Dido, who had committed suicide, in the Land of the Dead, but she had refused to even talk to him.

Antony called, "Come, Eros! Eros!"

Eros returned and asked, "What does my lord want?"

"Since Cleopatra died, I have lived in such dishonor that the gods detest my baseness. I, who with my sword divided the world into quarters, and over the back of the ocean, the domain of the god Neptune, made cities with my numerous ships, condemn myself because I lack the courage of a woman; I have a less noble mind than she, who by her death told Caesar, 'I am conqueror of myself.' By killing herself, she — not Caesar — conquered herself. You have sworn, Eros, that when the decisive moment should come, which indeed has now come — that time when I should look behind me and see disgrace and horror inevitably overtaking me — that, on my command, you then would kill me. Do what you promised to do; the time has come. You will strike me, but it is Caesar whom you defeat. Put color in your cheeks and gather the courage to do this."

"The gods forbid!" Eros said. "Shall I do that which all the Parthian darts, although hostile to you, could not do? None of the Parthian spears and arrows struck you."

"Eros, do you want to be located at a window in great Rome and see your master like this?" Antony demonstrated what he meant when he said, "Do you want to see your master with bent and tied arms, bending down his submissive neck, his face subdued and displaying the redness of shame, while the wheeled chariot of fortunate Caesar, drawn before him, marks like a brand the humiliation of me, who follows behind him?"

"I do not want to see that," Eros replied.

"Come, then; for with a wound I must be cured," Antony said. "Draw your honest sword, which you have worn most usefully for your country."

"Oh, sir, pardon me!"

"When I made you a free man, didn't you swear then to do this when I ordered you? Do it now, at once; or all your preceding services are only things that you did accidentally without intending to serve me. Draw your sword, and come and strike me."

"Turn away from me, then, your noble countenance to which the whole world pays homage."

"As you wish," Antony said, turning so that his back faced Eros.

"My sword is drawn," Eros said.

"Then do at once the thing for which you have drawn it."

"My dear master, my captain, and my Emperor, let me say, before I strike this bloody stroke, farewell."

"You have said it, man," Antony said. "And I say farewell to you."

"Farewell, great chief. Shall I strike now?" Eros asked.

"Now, Eros."

"Why, there then," Eros said, stabbing himself. "Thus I do escape the sorrow of Antony's death!"

Eros died.

Mark Antony said to himself, "Eros, you are thrice nobler than myself! You teach me, valiant Eros, to do what I should do, and what you could not — kill me. My Queen and Eros have by their brave example got before myself a noble spot in the history books, but I will be a bridegroom in my death, and run to death as if I were running to a lover's bed. Come, then; and, Eros, your master dies your scholar. I have learned from you how to do this."

Antony fell upon his sword. He gave himself a mortal wound, but he did not die immediately from it.

He said, "What! I am not dead? Not dead?"

He called, "Guards, come here! Oh, finish killing me!"

Dercetus, who was one of Mark Antony's followers, and some guards entered the room.

"What's that noise?" the first guard said.

Antony said, "I have done my work badly, friends. Oh, make an end of what I have begun."

"The Sun that lit our world has fallen," the second guard said.

"And his time is at its end," the first guard said.

The guards mourned.

"Let him who loves me strike me dead," Antony requested.

"Not I," the first guard said.

"Nor I," the second guard said.

"Nor anyone," the third guard said.

The guards left the room.

Dercetus said, "Your death and bad fortune are reasons for your followers to flee away from you."

He picked up Antony's sword and said, "If I show this sword to Octavius Caesar and bring him news of your death, Caesar will treat me well."

Diomedes, one of Cleopatra's servants, entered the room and asked Dercetus, "Where's Antony?"

"There he is, Diomedes," Dercetus replied, pointing. "There he is."

"Is he alive?" Diomedes asked.

Dercetus ignored him and left.

"Won't you answer me, man?" Diomedes asked.

Antony asked, "Is that you, Diomedes? Draw your sword, and give me sword strokes that will result in my death."

"Most absolute lord, my mistress — Cleopatra — sent me to you."

"When did she send you?"

"Just now, my lord."

"Where is she?"

"Locked in her monument," Diomedes replied. "She had a prophesying fear of what has come to pass. For when she saw that you suspected that she had made an agreement with Caesar — which shall never happen — and that your rage would not abate, she sent you a message that she was dead, but fearing what might result from that message, has sent me to proclaim the truth, but I have come, I fear, too late."

"Yes, you are too late, good Diomedes," Mark Antony said. "Call my guards, please."

"Guards! The Emperor's guards! The guards! Come here. Your lord wants you!"

Some of Antony's guards entered the room.

"Carry me, good friends, to where Cleopatra is staying; it is the last service that I shall command you to do for me."

"We grieve, sir," the first guard said, "that you will not outlive all your loyal followers."

"We grieve on this mournful day," the other guards said.

"No, my good fellows," Antony said. "Do not please sharp fate by gracing it with your sorrows; instead, welcome whatever comes to punish us — we punish it by seeming to bear it lightly. Pick me up. I have led you often. Carry me now, good friends, and I give my thanks for all you have done for me."

They carried Mark Antony away.

Cleopatra, Charmian, and Iras were at Cleopatra's monument. They were on a second-floor balcony.

"Oh, Charmian, I will never leave here," Cleopatra mourned.

"Be comforted, dear madam," Charmian replied.

"No, I will not," Cleopatra said. Using the royal plural, she added, "All strange and terrible events are welcome, but comforts we despise; the size of our sorrow must be in proportion to its cause — our sorrow must be as great as that which causes it."

Below the balcony appeared Diomedes.

Seeing him, Cleopatra asked, "What has happened? Is Antony dead?"

"He will die soon, but he is not dead yet," Diomedes replied. "Look over there. His guards have carried him here."

Cleopatra looked and saw Mark Antony being carried to her by his guards.

She said, "Oh, Sun, burn the great sphere that you move in! Escape from the sphere and leave and let the world with its days and nights and its tides be always dark."

According to Ptolemaic astronomy, the Sun and the planets were fixed in spheres that moved around the Earth, which was the center of the universe.

Cleopatra continued, "Oh, Antony, Antony, Antony! Help, Charmian! Help, Iras, help! Help, friends below! Let's draw him up here!"

"Quiet," Antony said. "Caesar's valor has not overthrown Antony, but Antony's valor has triumphed on itself. Caesar has not killed me; I have killed myself."

"That is as it should be," Cleopatra said. "No one but Antony should conquer Antony, but I still mourn that this happened!"

"I am dying, Queen of Egypt, dying," Mark Antony said, "but I ask death to wait awhile, until I lay on your lips the poor last of many thousand kisses."

"I dare not come down to you, dear — my dear lord, pardon me — I dare not, lest I be captured," Cleopatra said. "The imperious show of the good-fortuned Caesar never shall be decorated with me — I will not take an ignoble role in his triumphal procession in Rome. As long as knife, drugs, and serpents have edge, effect, or sting, I am safe. Your wife, Octavia, with her modest eyes and impassive judgment shall acquire no honor by looking smugly at me. But come to me, come, Antony — help me, my women — we must draw you up here. Help, good friends."

"Be quick; soon I will be dead."

Cleopatra and her female servants began to pull Antony up to the balcony.

"Here's work indeed!" Cleopatra said. "How heavy is my lord! Our strength has all disappeared because of the heaviness of sorrow. If I had the great goddess Juno's power, the strong-winged Mercury should fetch you up to Heaven, and set you by the side of Jove, King of the gods. We must lift you a little higher — mere wishing is foolish — oh, come, come, come."

They succeeded in raising Antony to the balcony.

"Welcome, welcome!" Cleopatra said. "Die where you have lived. Come to life with my kisses. If my lips had that power, I would wear them out like this."

She kissed Mark Antony several times.

This is a heavy and sad sight, the people around her thought.

"I am dying, Queen of Egypt, dying," Mark Antony said. "Give me some wine, and let me speak a little."

"No, let me speak; and let me curse so vehemently that the false hussy Fortune will break her wheel because she is so angered by my curses."

"One word, sweet Queen," Antony said. "From Caesar seek your honor, along with your safety."

"My honor and my safety do not go together," Cleopatra replied.

"Noble lady, listen to me," Antony said. "Trust none of Caesar's men except Proculeius."

"I will trust my resolution and my hands, but I will trust none of Caesar's men."

"The miserable change of fortune I suffer now at the end of my life neither lament nor sorrow at, but please your thoughts by remembering my former good fortune when I lived as the greatest Prince of the world, and the noblest. Also know that I do not now basely die. I have not cowardly taken off my helmet and submitted myself to Caesar, my countryman. Instead, I am a Roman who by a Roman — myself — is valiantly vanquished. By committing suicide, I have conquered myself. Now my spirit is going; I can say no more."

"Noblest of men, will you die?" Cleopatra asked. "Don't you care about me! Shall I live in this dull world, which in your absence is no better than a pigsty? Oh, look, my women!"

Mark Antony died.

"The crown of the Earth melts," Cleopatra said. "My lord! Oh, withered is the garland of the war. The soldier's standard has fallen; young boys and girls are equal now with men; the marks of distinction are gone, and nothing remarkable is left beneath the visiting moon."

Cleopatra fainted.

"Oh, be calm, lady!" Charmian said.

"Our Queen has died, too," Iras said.

"Lady!" Charmian said.

"Madam!" Iras said.

"Oh, madam, madam, madam!" Charmian said.

"Royal Queen of Egypt!" Iras said. "Empress!"

Cleopatra regained consciousness.

"Quiet! Quiet, Iras!" Charmian said.

Cleopatra said, "I am no more than just a woman, and I am ruled by such poor passion as rules the maid who milks and does the meanest chores. It would be fitting for me to throw my scepter at the injurious and harm-doing gods and tell them that this world was the equal of theirs until they stole Mark Antony, our jewel. Nothing matters anymore. Staying calm is foolish, and being angry is fitting for a mad dog. Is it then a sin to hurry into the secret house of Death before Death dares come to us? How are you, women? Tell me! Be of good cheer! Why, how are you now, Charmian! My noble girls! Ah, women, women, look, our lamp is spent — it's out!

"Good ladies, take heart: We'll bury him; and then, what's brave, what's noble, let's do it after the high Roman fashion, and make Death proud to take us."

She was thinking of committing suicide.

She added, "Come, let's go away. This corpse that contained that huge spirit is now cold. Ah, women, women! Come; we have no friend but resolution, and the quickest possible end of life."

CHAPTER 5

— 5.1 —

In Octavius Caesar's camp before Alexandria, Caesar was meeting with Agrippa, Dolabella, Maecenas, Gallus, Proculeius, and others in a council of war.

Caesar ordered, "Go to Mark Antony, Dolabella, and order him to surrender. Tell him that since he has been so badly defeated, he is embarrassing himself by delaying his surrender."

"Caesar, I shall," Dolabella said and then exited.

Dercetus, carrying Mark Antony's bloody sword, now walked over to Caesar.

Caesar said, "What is the meaning of this? Who are you who dares to appear before me while you are carrying an unsheathed sword?"

"I am named Dercetus. I served Mark Antony, who was most worthy to be best served. While he stood up and spoke, he was my master; and I was willing to lose my life fighting his haters. I was willing to die for him. If you please to take me into your service, I will be to Caesar what I was to him. If you do not want to take me into your service, then I surrender my life to you."

"What are you saying?" Caesar asked.

"I say, Caesar, that Antony is dead."

"The breaking of so great a thing should make a greater noise," Caesar said. "Thunder and an earthquake should occur. The round world should have shaken lions into city streets, and citizens should have been shaken into the lions' dens. The death of Antony is not a single fate; Antony controlled half of the world."

"He is dead, Caesar," Dercetus said, "not by a public minister of justice, nor by a hired knife; but he has, by that selfsame hand that wrote his honor in the acts it did and with the courage that his heart lent it, split his heart. This is Antony's sword — I robbed his wound of it. Look, his sword is stained with Antony's most noble blood."

"Look, sad friends," Caesar said, pointing to the sword. "The gods may rebuke me for mourning, but these are tidings to wash with tears the eyes of Kings."

"How strange it is," Agrippa said, "that our human nature compels us to lament the result of actions we pursued most persistently."

Maecenas said, "Antony's bad and good points were equally matched."

"A rarer spirit never steered humanity," Agrippa said, "but the gods always give us some faults that make us fallible men. Caesar is touched by Antony's death."

Maecenas said, "When such a spacious mirror as Antony is set before him, Caesar must necessarily see himself in the mirror."

"Oh, Antony!" Octavius Caesar said. "I have pursued you to this catastrophe, but we lance diseases in our bodies to cure them. I was forced to either show you my own such catastrophe or look on yours. You and I could not live together in this world, but still let me lament you, with tears as sovereign as the blood of hearts, my brother, my partner and competitor in the most exalted enterprises, my mate in empire, my friend and companion in the front lines of war, the arm of my own body, and the heart where my heart kindles its thoughts of courage — let me lament that our stars, which could not be reconciled, should divide us and bring us to this conclusion. Hear me, good friends —"

Caesar saw an Egyptian messenger arriving, so he said, "But I will tell you at some more suitable time. This man has obviously come on important business. We will hear what he says."

Caesar asked, "Where have you come from?"

"I have come from one who is still a poor Egyptian," the messenger replied.

He was aware that soon Egypt would become a Roman province and would be no longer a sovereign nation.

He continued, "Queen Cleopatra is shut up in the only thing she has left: her monument, which is her tomb. She wishes to know what you intend to do so that she may prepare herself to bend the way she is forced to."

"Tell her to have courage," Caesar said. "She soon shall know, by some messengers of ours, how honorably and how kindly we will treat her; Caesar cannot live as an ignoble person."

"May the gods preserve you!" the Egyptian messenger replied, and then he exited.

Using the royal plural, Caesar said, "Come here, Proculeius. Go to Cleopatra and say that we intend to give her no shame. Give to her whatever comforts and comforting words are necessary to keep her, in her grief, from defeating us by giving herself mortal wounds and committing suicide. If we can keep her alive and have her appear in our triumphal procession in Rome, the memory of my triumph will be eternal. Go, and as quickly as you can come back and tell us what she says and what you can learn about her."

"Caesar, I shall," Proculeius said, and then he exited.

"Gallus, go with him," Caesar ordered.

Gallus exited.

Caesar asked, "Where's Dolabella? He should assist Proculeius."

"Dolabella!" the others called.

"Let him alone," Caesar said. "I remember now that he is elsewhere employed. He shall return in time to be ready for this job."

He added, "Go with me to my tent, where you shall see how reluctantly I was drawn into this war. I always proceeded calmly and gently in all my letters to Antony. Come with me, and see the letters I will show to you."

Cleopatra, Charmian, and Iras were in a room in Cleopatra's monument.

Cleopatra said, "My desolation begins to make a better life. It is paltry to be Caesar; he is not Fortune, but only Fortune's servant: a minister of her will."

She added, "It is great to do that thing that ends all other deeds. That thing stops accidents and changes from happening, that thing sleeps, and that thing never again tastes food from the earth — food that feeds both the beggar's nurse and Caesar's nurse."

Proculeius arrived.

Proculeius said, "Caesar sends greetings to the Queen of Egypt, and he asks you to think about what fair requests you want to have him grant you."

"What's your name?" Cleopatra asked.

"My name is Proculeius."

"Antony told me about you. He told me to trust you, but I have little risk of being deceived, since I will not trust anyone. If your master wants a Queen to be his beggar, you must tell him that majesty, to keep up appearances, must beg for no less than a Kingdom. If he will give me conquered Egypt so I can give it to my son, he gives me so much of what is my own that I will kneel to him with thanks."

"Be of good cheer," Proculeius said. "You've fallen into a Princely hand. Fear nothing. Give your fate freely to my lord, who is so full of grace that it flows over onto all who are in need. Let me report to him that you are willingly dependent on him and you shall find that he is a conqueror who will ask you how he can be kind to those who kneel before him and ask him for grace."

"Please tell him that I am a vassal to his good fortune, and I send to him the greatness that he has earned. Each hour I learn how to be obedient, and I would gladly meet with him."

"This I'll report, dear lady," Proculeius replied. "Have comfort because I know that your plight is pitied by him who caused it."

Gallus and some Roman soldiers entered the room.

Gallus said, "You see how easily Cleopatra may be surprised and captured."

He said to the soldiers, "Guard her until Caesar comes."

"Royal Queen!" Iras said.

"Oh, Cleopatra!" Charmian said. "You have been captured, Queen."

"Be quick, quick, my good hands," Cleopatra said, drawing a dagger and intending to kill herself.

"Stop, worthy lady, stop," Proculeius said, taking the dagger forcefully away from her. "Don't do yourself such wrong. In this you are rescued, not betrayed."

"Rescued from death?" Cleopatra said. "Rescued from the thing that keeps our dogs from suffering a lingering illness?"

"Cleopatra," Proculeius said, "do not abuse my master's bounty by killing yourself. Let the world see Caesar displaying his nobleness and generosity to you. If you die, he will not be able to display those qualities to you."

"Where are you, Death?" Cleopatra asked. "Come here, come! Come, come, and take a Queen who is worth many babes and beggars — your easiest conquests!"

"Control yourself, lady," Proculeius said.

"Sir, I will eat no food," Cleopatra said. "I will not drink, sir. If idle talk will once be necessary, I will not talk. I will not sleep, either. This mortal house — my body — I'll ruin, no matter what Caesar does to try to stop me. Know, sir, that I will not wait, bound, at your master's court, nor ever be chastised by the sober eye of dull Octavia. Shall they hoist me up in a triumphal procession and display me to the shouting commoners of censuring Rome? I prefer that a ditch in Egypt be my gentle grave! I prefer to lie stark naked on the mud of the Nile River and let the water-flies lay their eggs in or on my skin, causing my body to swell up and become abhorrent! I prefer to make my country's high obelisks my gibbet, where I will be hanged up in chains!"

"Your thoughts of horror go way beyond anything that Caesar shall give you cause to think," Proculeius said.

Dolabella entered the room and said, "Proculeius, your master, Caesar, knows what you have done, and he has sent for you. As for the Queen, I will guard her."

"This is good, Dolabella," Proculeius said. "Be gentle to her."

Proculeius said to Cleopatra, "I will tell Caesar whatever message you want to give him, if you want me to serve as your messenger."

"Tell him that I want to die."

Proculeius and the Roman soldiers exited, leaving behind Dolabella, Cleopatra, Charmian, and Iras.

"Most noble Empress, have you heard of me?" Dolabella asked.

"I cannot tell."

"I am sure that you know about me."

"It does not matter, sir, what I have heard or known," Cleopatra replied. "You laugh when boys or women tell their dreams — isn't that your custom?"

"I don't understand, madam," Dolabella replied.

"I dreamed that an Emperor Antony existed," Cleopatra said. "Oh, I wish that I could sleep another such sleep, so that I might see another such man!"

"If it might please you —" Dolabella began.

Cleopatra interrupted, "His face was like the Heavens; and in his face were a Sun and a Moon, which kept their course, and lighted the little O — the Earth."

"Most sovereign creature —" Dolabella began.

Cleopatra continued: "His legs bestrode the ocean. His reared arm dominated the world. His voice had the properties of all the tuned spheres, and he sounded like the music of the spheres when he talked to friends, but when he meant to make the world quail and shake, his voice was like rattling thunder. As for his bounty, it had no winter; his bounty was like an autumn with a bountiful harvest — autumn is the season of plenty. His delights were dolphin-like; they showed his back above the element they lived in — he was like a dolphin whose enjoyment of the sea it lives in causes it to swim energetically and raise its back above the surface of the sea. Among his servants were Kings and Princes. Realms and islands were like coins that dropped from his pocket."

"Cleopatra!" Dolabella said.

"Do you think there was, or might be, such a man as this man I dreamed about?"

"Gentle madam, no."

"You lie, and the gods hear you lie," Cleopatra said. "But, if there is, or ever were, a man such as he, his greatness would be too much to dream about. Nature lacks the material to create strange forms that can compete with those made by our imagination. Yet, if Nature could make an image of an Antony, it would be Nature's masterpiece and it would surpass imagination — it would quite surpass imaginary beings."

"Listen to me, good madam," Dolabella said. "Your loss is like yourself — great — and you bear it appropriately for its greatness. I wish that I might never achieve the success I pursue unless I feel, in empathy for your grief, a grief that smites my very heart at its root."

"I thank you, sir," Cleopatra said. "Do you know what Caesar means to do with me?"

"I am loath to tell you what I wish you knew," Dolabella said.

"Please tell me, sir."

"Although Caesar is honorable —"

"— he'll lead me, then, in triumph?"

"Madam, he will," Dolabella said. "I know he will."

The sound of a trumpet was heard, and Octavius Caesar, Gallus, Proculeius, Maecenas, and other followers of Caesar entered the room.

"Which is the Queen of Egypt?" Caesar asked.

Dolabella said to Cleopatra, "This is the Emperor, madam."

This was a way for Dolabella to show respect to Cleopatra. Caesar had stated that he did not know which woman was Cleopatra. Dolabella had therefore pretended that Cleopatra did not know this man is Caesar.

Cleopatra knelt before Caesar.

"Arise, you shall not kneel," Caesar said. "Please, rise; rise, Queen of Egypt."

"Sir, the gods will have it thus," Cleopatra replied. "I must obey my master and my lord."

She stood up.

"Think no hard thoughts," Caesar said to her. "The record of those injuries you did to us, although they are written as scars in our flesh, we shall remember as injuries done by accident and chance."

"Sole ruler of the world," Cleopatra said. "I cannot state my own case so well as to make it clear and innocent, but I do confess that I have the frailties that often have previously shamed women."

Caesar said, using the royal plural, "Cleopatra, know that we will forgive rather than punish if you do what we ask of you. Our intentions towards you are most gentle, and you shall find it to your benefit to conform with our will, but if you seek to give me a reason to be cruel by your taking Antony's course and committing suicide, you shall bereave yourself of my good intentions, and bring destruction to your children — destruction from which I'll guard them if you will rely on me. I'll take my leave."

Caesar wanted to leave, but Cleopatra kept talking.

"You may take your leave — and do whatever you want — throughout the world," Cleopatra said. "The world is yours; and we are your signs of conquest. We are like the shields of enemy warriors that you hang in whatever place you please."

The word "hang" referred both to the shields and to the enemy warriors.

She handed him a document and said, "Here, my good lord."

"You shall advise me in everything that concerns Cleopatra," Caesar said to her.

"This document is a list of the money, plate, and jewels that I possess. It is exactly valued, except that it does not list petty things. Where's Seleucus?"

He entered the room and said, "Here I am, madam."

"This is my treasurer," Cleopatra said to Caesar. "Let him testify, my lord, upon his peril, that I have reserved nothing for myself. Speak the truth, Seleucus."

"Madam," he said to Cleopatra, "I would rather seal my lips, than, to my peril, speak that which is not true."

"What have I kept back for myself? What of value does not appear in this list?" Cleopatra asked.

"Enough to purchase what appears on that list."

Caesar was amused. He also felt that this was a sign that Cleopatra wished to continue to live.

"Don't blush, Cleopatra," he said. "I approve of your wisdom in holding back some valuables for yourself."

"See, Caesar!" Cleopatra complained. "See how pomp is followed! My followers will now be yours; and, if we should change positions, your followers would be mine. The ingratitude of this Seleucus makes me completely wild."

She said to Seleucus, "Oh, slave. You can be no more trusted than a love who's hired — a prostitute! What, are you fleeing from me? You have reason to flee from me, I promise you, but I'll scratch your eyes even if they have wings to flee from me, you slave, you soulless villain, you dog! You are an exceptionally base man!"

"Good Queen, let us entreat you —" Caesar began.

Cleopatra interrupted, "Oh, Caesar, what a wounding shame is this. You condescended to visit me here, you gave the honor of your lordliness to me, one who is so meek, and my own envious servant increased the sum of my disgraces.

Let us say, good Caesar, that I have reserved some feminine trifles, unimportant toys, things of such dignity as we give to everyday friends; and let us say that a few nobler tokens I have kept off the list of my possessions so that I can give them to your wife, Livia, and to Octavia to induce them to help me. Let us say these things. Does it follow that a servant of my own household must reveal to you my actions? The gods! I have already fallen so far, and this causes me to fall further."

She said to Seleucus, "Please, go away from here. If you don't, I shall show the cinders of my spirits through the ashes of my fortune. Despite my misfortunes, I still have a little spirit left. If you were a man, you would have had mercy on me."

"Leave us, Seleucus," Caesar ordered.

Seleucus exited.

"People need to realize that we, the greatest, are thought, mistakenly, to be responsible for things that other people do, and, when we fall in fortune, we answer for that. Therefore, people should feel pity for us when other people, such as Seleucus, try to get credit at the expense of the good names of the greatest."

"Cleopatra, neither what you have reserved for yourself, nor what you have acknowledged in your list of possessions, will be part of our spoils of war. These possessions still belong to you; do with them whatever you wish. Believe that I, Caesar, am not a merchant who will haggle with you about the things that merchants sell. Therefore, be cheerful. Do not let gloomy thoughts imprison you. No, dear Queen; we intend to treat you as you yourself shall advise us. Eat, and sleep. We care for you and pity you very much, and we remain your friend, and so, *adieu*."

"My master, and my lord!" Cleopatra said.

"I am neither," Caesar replied. "*Adieu*."

Octavius Caesar, Gallus, Proculeius, Maecenas, Dolabella, and the other followers of Caesar exited, leaving behind Cleopatra, Charmian, and Iras.

"Caesar words me, girls, he words me," Cleopatra said. "He is saying these things so that I will not be noble to myself and commit suicide."

She said, "Listen, Charmian," and whispered in her ear.

"End your life, good lady," Iras said. "The bright day is done, and we are going into the dark."

"Hurry once more," Cleopatra said to Charmian. "I have given my orders already, and what I need has been acquired. Run this errand quickly."

"Madam, I will," Charmian said.

Dolabella came back into the room and asked, "Where is the Queen?"

"There she is, sir," Charmian said, pointing to Cleopatra, and then she exited.

"Dolabella!" Cleopatra said.

"As I promised you," Dolabella said, "something that my respect for you made me do, I have found out the information you wanted. Caesar intends to journey through Syria, and within three days he will send you and your children ahead of him. Make the best use you can of this information. I have done what you wanted and what I promised to do."

"Dolabella, I shall remain your debtor," Cleopatra said.

"I am your servant," Dolabella replied. "*Adieu*, good Queen; I must attend on Caesar."

"Farewell, and thanks."

Dolabella exited.

"Now, Iras," Cleopatra said. "What do you think? You, as if you were an Egyptian puppet, shall be shown in a triumphal procession in Rome, as well as I. Rude workmen with greasy aprons, rulers, and hammers shall lift us up so that we can be seen. Their thick breaths, which stink because of their poor diet, will make clouds around us, and we will be forced to breathe the vapor inside us."

"The gods forbid!" Iras said.

"This is most certain to occur, Iras," Cleopatra said. "Lecherous bailiffs will grab at us as if we were prostitutes; and scabby rhymers will ballad us out of tune. The quick-witted comedians will perform us in impromptu plays and present our Alexandrian revels; they will act the role of Antony as if he were a drunken alcoholic, and I shall see some squeaking boy act the role of the great Cleopatra as if she were a whore."

"Oh, the good gods!" Iras said.

"These things are sure to happen," Cleopatra said.

"I'll never see them because I am sure that my fingernails are stronger than my eyes," Iras said.

"Why, that's the way to foil their scheming plans, and to conquer their most absurd intentions," Cleopatra said.

Charmian entered the room.

"Charmian!" Cleopatra said. "My women, make me look like a Queen. Go and fetch my best clothing. I am once again — metaphorically — going to the Cydnus River to meet Mark Antony. Iras, go and fetch my clothing."

Iras exited.

"Now, noble Charmian," Cleopatra said, "we'll get things over and done with, indeed. And, when you have done this chore, I'll give you leave to play until Doomsday — the Day of Judgment."

Using the royal plural, she said, "Bring to us our crown and all that goes with it."

Hearing something, she asked, "What is that noise?"

A guard entered the room and said, "A rural fellow who will not be kept from your Highness' presence insists on seeing you. He brings you figs."

"Let him come in," Cleopatra said.

The guard exited to carry out the request.

"How poor an instrument may do a noble deed!" Cleopatra said. "He brings me liberty. My resolution's fixed, and I have nothing of woman in me — I am not weak. Now from head to foot I am as unchanging as marble; now the fleeting and changing Moon is no planet of mine."

The guard entered the room, leading a farmer who carried a basket.

"This is the man," the guard said.

"Go, and leave him here," Cleopatra said.

The guard exited.

"Have you the pretty snake of the Nile there, the snake that kills without causing pain?" Cleopatra asked.

The pretty snake of the Nile was an asp. Its poison caused the victim to feel sleepy and then die.

"Yes, I have it," the farmer said, "but I would not be the party who should desire you to touch it, for its bite is immortal; those who die of it seldom or never recover."

The farmer often misused words. He had said "immortal," but he had meant "mortal."

"Do you remember anyone who has died from its bite?"

"Very many, both men and women," the farmer replied. "I heard about one of them no longer ago than yesterday. She was a very honest woman, but somewhat given to lie, as a woman should not do, except in the way of honesty."

The farmer's words had an additional meaning. "Lie" could be understood as "lie with a man," and "honest" could meant "chaste," so the farmer was saying, "She was a very honest woman, but somewhat given to lie with a man, as a woman should not do, except with her husband."

The farmer continued: "I heard how she died of the snake's bite and what pain she felt; truly, she made a very good report concerning the snake, but he who will believe all that women say shall never be saved by half that women do, but this is most fallible, this snake's an odd snake."

The farmer had misused another word. He had said "fallible," but he had meant "infallible."

"Go now," Cleopatra said. "Farewell."

"I hope that you will satisfied with the snake," the farmer replied.

He set down his basket but did not leave.

"Farewell," Cleopatra said.

"You must know something," the farmer said. "You must understand that the snake will do what a snake does — it will bite."

"Yes, yes," Cleopatra said. "Farewell."

"Know that the snake is not to be trusted except in the keeping of people who know how to deal with snakes because, indeed, there is no goodness in a snake."

"Don't worry about that," Cleopatra said. "I will be careful."

"Very good. Give it nothing to eat, please, because it is not worth the feeding."

"Will it eat me?" Cleopatra asked. She wanted the snake to bite her.

"You must not think I am so simple that I don't know the Devil himself will not eat a woman," the farmer said. "I know that a woman is a dish for the gods, if the Devil does not dress her for the table. But, truly, these same whoreson Devils do the gods great harm when it comes to women; for out of every ten women that the gods make, the Devils mar five."

"Well, leave now," Cleopatra said. "Farewell."

"Yes, indeed," the farmer said. "I hope that you are pleased with the snake."

The farmer exited as Iras returned, carrying Cleopatra's royal robe, crown, and other items.

"Give me my robe, and put my crown on me," Cleopatra said. "I have longings in me to be immortal. I shall never again drink the wine of Egypt."

Charmian and Iras began to dress her.

"Smartly, smartly, good Iras; be quick," Cleopatra said. "I think I hear Antony calling me. I see him rouse himself to praise my noble act. I hear him mock the luck of Caesar, which the gods give men to excuse their wrath to come. Those whom the gods would destroy, they first make fortunate. Husband, I am coming. Let my courage prove that I deserve the title of Antony's wife! I am fire and air; my other elements — earth and water — I give to baser life. Are you done dressing me? Come then, and take the last warmth of my lips. Farewell, kind Charmian; Iras, farewell for a long time."

Cleopatra kissed both of them, and Iras dropped dead from grief.

Cleopatra said, "Have I the poison of the asp on my lips? Have you fallen? If you and Nature can so gently part, the stroke of death is like a lover's pinch, which hurts, and which is desired. Do you lie still? If you vanish like this from the earth, you tell the world it is not worth saying farewell to."

Charmian said, "Dissolve, thick cloud, and rain, so that I may say that the gods themselves are weeping!"

"This thought I have proves that I am base," Cleopatra said. "If Iras meets Antony with his curled hair before I do, he will demand a kiss from her and spend that kiss that is my Heaven to have."

She withdrew an asp from the basket and held it to her breast and said, "Come, you mortal wretch, with your sharp teeth immediately untie this intricate knot of life. You poor venomous fool, be angry and dispatch me. Oh, I wish that you could speak so that I could hear you call great Caesar a politically outmaneuvered ass!"

By killing herself, Cleopatra was frustrating Octavius Caesar's plans to force her to be in his triumphal procession in Rome.

"Oh, Eastern star!" Charmian said. She was calling Cleopatra Venus.

"Silence! Silence!" Cleopatra said. "Do you not see my baby at my breast, sucking the nurse so that she will fall asleep?"

"Oh, my heart, break!" Charmian said.

"As sweet as balm, as soft as air, as gentle — oh, Antony!" Cleopatra said.

She took another snake from the basket and held it to her arm, saying, "I will take you, too. Why should I stay —"

Cleopatra died.

Charmian finished the sentence for her: "— in this vile world? So, fare you well. Now, Death, boast. In your possession lies an unparalleled lass."

She closed Cleopatra's eyelids and said, "Soft eyes, close. Golden Phoebus — the Sun — will never be beheld again by eyes so royal! Your crown's awry. I'll straighten it, and then play."

Some guards rushed into the room.

The first guard said, "Where is the Queen?"

"Speak softly," Charmian replied. "Don't wake her."

The first guard said, "Caesar has sent —"

Charmian finished the sentence: "— too slow a messenger."

She held an asp to her arm and said, "Oh, Death. Come quickly; hurry! I partly feel you."

The first guard called, "Come here! All's not well! Caesar's been fooled."

The second guard said, "Dolabella was sent here from Caesar; call him."

"What deed is this!" the first guard said. "Charmian, is this well done?"

"It is well done," she replied, "and this deed is fitting for a Princess descended from so many royal Kings. Ah, soldier!"

Charmian died.

Dolabella came into the room and asked, "What is going on here?"

The second guard replied, "Everyone is dead."

Dolabella said, "Caesar, your suspicions have come true in this room. You yourself are coming to see performed the dreaded act that you so sought to stop."

Outside the room came cries: "Make way for Caesar! Make a path for Caesar!"

Octavius Caesar and others entered the room.

Dolabella said to Caesar, "Oh, sir, you are too accurate an augur; that which you feared would happen has happened."

"Bravest at the end, Cleopatra guessed at our purposes, and, being royal, she took her own way," Caesar said. "How did they die? I do not see them bleed."

"Who was the last person to be with them?" Dolabella asked.

"A simple farmer, who brought her figs," the first guard said. He pointed and added, "This was his basket."

"They were poisoned, then," Caesar said.

"Oh, Caesar," the first guard said. "Charmian was alive just now; she stood and spoke. I found her straightening the diadem on her dead mistress. Tremblingly, Charmian stood and then suddenly dropped to the floor."

"Women are weak, but these women were noble," Caesar said. "If they had swallowed poison, we would know it because their bodies would be swollen, but Cleopatra looks like she is sleeping. She looks as if she would catch another Antony in her strong net of grace."

Dolabella said, "Here, on her breast, there are small holes and a trickling of blood. The same is true of her arm."

"This is an asp's trail," the first guard said, "and these fig-leaves have slime upon them, such as the asp leaves in the caves of the Nile."

"Most probably Cleopatra died from the asp's bite," Caesar said, "for her physician tells me she had pursued innumerable experiments to find easy ways to die. Pick up her bed; and carry her dead women servants from the monument. She shall be buried by her Antony. No grave upon the earth shall embrace in it a pair of lovers as famous as these two. Tragic catastrophes such as these distress those who cause them; and their story is no less in pity than is the glory of the man who caused them to be lamented. Our army shall in solemn show attend this funeral, and then we shall go to Rome. Dolabella, ensure that this great ceremony is conducted with dignified splendor."

Appendix A: About the Author

It was a dark and stormy night. Suddenly a cry rang out, and on a hot summer night in 1954, Josephine, wife of Carl Bruce, gave birth to a boy — me. Unfortunately, this young married couple allowed Reuben Saturday, Josephine's brother, to name their first-born. Reuben, aka "The Joker," decided that Bruce was a nice name, so he decided to name me Bruce Bruce. I have gone by my middle name — David — ever since.

Being named Bruce David Bruce hasn't been all bad. Bank tellers remember me very quickly, so I don't often have to show an ID. It can be fun in charades, also. When I was a counselor as a teenager at Camp Echoing Hills in Warsaw, Ohio, a fellow counselor gave the signs for "sounds like" and "two words," then she pointed to a bruise on her leg twice. Bruise Bruise? Oh yeah, Bruce Bruce is the answer!

Uncle Reuben, by the way, gave me a haircut when I was in kindergarten. He cut my hair short and shaved a small bald spot on the back of my head. My mother wouldn't let me go to school until the bald spot grew out again.

Of all my brothers and sisters (six in all), I am the only transplant to Athens, Ohio. I was born in Newark, Ohio, and have lived all around Southeastern Ohio. However, I moved to Athens to go to Ohio University and have never left.

At Ohio U, I never could make up my mind whether to major in English or Philosophy, so I got a bachelor's degree with a double major in both areas, then I added a Master's of Arts degree in English and a Master's of Arts degree in Philosophy. Yes, I have my MAMA degree.

Currently, and for a long time to come (I eat fruits and veggies), I am spending my retirement writing books such as *Nadia Comaneci: Perfect 10*, *The Funniest People in Dance*, *Homer's* Iliad: *A Retelling in Prose*, and *William Shakespeare's* Othello: *A Retelling in Prose*.

By the way, my sister Brenda Kennedy writes romances such as *A New Beginning* and *Shattered Dreams*.

Appendix B: Some Books by David Bruce

Retellings of a Classic Work of Literature

Arden of Faversham: *A Retelling*

Ben Jonson's The Alchemist: *A Retelling*

Ben Jonson's The Arraignment, or Poetaster: *A Retelling*

Ben Jonson's Bartholomew Fair: *A Retelling*

Ben Jonson's The Case is Altered: *A Retelling*

Ben Jonson's Catiline's Conspiracy: *A Retelling*

Ben Jonson's The Devil is an Ass: *A Retelling*

Ben Jonson's Epicene: *A Retelling*

Ben Jonson's Every Man in His Humor: *A Retelling*

Ben Jonson's Every Man Out of His Humor: *A Retelling*

Ben Jonson's The Fountain of Self-Love, or Cynthia's Revels: *A Retelling*

Ben Jonson's The Magnetic Lady, or Humors Reconciled: *A Retelling*

Ben Jonson's The New Inn, or The Light Heart: *A Retelling*

Ben Jonson's Sejanus' Fall: *A Retelling*

Ben Jonson's The Staple of News: *A Retelling*

Ben Jonson's A Tale of a Tub: *A Retelling*

Ben Jonson's Volpone, or the Fox: *A Retelling*

Christopher Marlowe's Complete Plays: Retellings

Christopher Marlowe's Dido, Queen of Carthage: *A Retelling*

Christopher Marlowe's Doctor Faustus: *Retellings of the 1604 A-Text and of the 1616 B-Text*

Christopher Marlowe's Edward II: *A Retelling*

Christopher Marlowe's The Massacre at Paris: *A Retelling*

Christopher Marlowe's The Rich Jew of Malta: *A Retelling*

Christopher Marlowe's Tamburlaine, Parts 1 and 2: *Retellings*

Dante's Divine Comedy: *A Retelling in Prose*

Dante's Inferno: *A Retelling in Prose*

Dante's Purgatory: *A Retelling in Prose*

Dante's Paradise: *A Retelling in Prose*

The Famous Victories of Henry V: *A Retelling*

From the Iliad *to the* Odyssey: *A Retelling in Prose of Quintus of Smyrna's* Posthomerica

George Chapman, Ben Jonson, and John Marston's Eastward Ho! *A Retelling*

George Peele's The Arraignment of Paris: *A Retelling*

George Peele's The Battle of Alcazar: *A Retelling*

George's Peele's David and Bathsheba, and the Tragedy of Absalom: *A Retelling*

George Peele's Edward I: *A Retelling*

George Peele's The Old Wives' Tale: *A Retelling*

George-a-Greene: *A Retelling*

The History of King Leir: *A Retelling*
Homer's Iliad: *A Retelling in Prose*
Homer's Odyssey: *A Retelling in Prose*
J.W. Gent.'s The Valiant Scot: *A Retelling*
Jason and the Argonauts: A Retelling in Prose of Apollonius of Rhodes' Argonautica
John Ford: Eight Plays Translated into Modern English
John Ford's The Broken Heart: *A Retelling*
John Ford's The Fancies, Chaste and Noble: *A Retelling*
John Ford's The Lady's Trial: *A Retelling*
John Ford's The Lover's Melancholy: *A Retelling*
John Ford's Love's Sacrifice: *A Retelling*
John Ford's Perkin Warbeck: *A Retelling*
John Ford's The Queen: *A Retelling*
John Ford's 'Tis Pity She's a Whore: *A Retelling*
John Lyly's Campaspe: *A Retelling*
John Lyly's Endymion, The Man in the Moon: *A Retelling*
John Lyly's Galatea: *A Retelling*
John Lyly's Love's Metamorphosis: *A Retelling*
John Lyly's Midas: *A Retelling*
John Lyly's Mother Bombie: *A Retelling*
John Lyly's Sappho and Phao: *A Retelling*
John Lyly's The Woman in the Moon: *A Retelling*
John Webster's The White Devil: *A Retelling*
King Edward III: *A Retelling*
Mankind: *A Medieval Morality Play* (A Retelling)
Margaret Cavendish's The Unnatural Tragedy: *A Retelling*
The Merry Devil of Edmonton: *A Retelling*
The Summoning of Everyman: *A Medieval Morality Play* (A Retelling)
Robert Greene's Friar Bacon and Friar Bungay: *A Retelling*
The Taming of a Shrew: *A Retelling*
Tarlton's Jests: A Retelling
Thomas Middleton's A Chaste Maid in Cheapside: *A Retelling*
Thomas Middleton's Women Beware Women: *A Retelling*
Thomas Middleton and Thomas Dekker's The Roaring Girl: *A Retelling*
Thomas Middleton and William Rowley's The Changeling: *A Retelling*
The Trojan War and Its Aftermath: Four Ancient Epic Poems
Virgil's Aeneid: *A Retelling in Prose*
William Shakespeare's 5 Late Romances: Retellings in Prose
William Shakespeare's 10 Histories: Retellings in Prose
William Shakespeare's 11 Tragedies: Retellings in Prose
William Shakespeare's 12 Comedies: Retellings in Prose
William Shakespeare's 38 Plays: Retellings in Prose

William Shakespeare's 1 Henry IV, aka Henry IV, Part 1: *A Retelling in Prose*

William Shakespeare's 2 Henry IV, aka Henry IV, Part 2: *A Retelling in Prose*

William Shakespeare's 1 Henry VI, aka Henry VI, Part 1: *A Retelling in Prose*

William Shakespeare's 2 Henry VI, aka Henry VI, Part 2: *A Retelling in Prose*

William Shakespeare's 3 Henry VI, aka Henry VI, Part 3: *A Retelling in Prose*

William Shakespeare's All's Well that Ends Well: *A Retelling in Prose*

William Shakespeare's Antony and Cleopatra: *A Retelling in Prose*

William Shakespeare's As You Like It: *A Retelling in Prose*

William Shakespeare's The Comedy of Errors: *A Retelling in Prose*

William Shakespeare's Coriolanus: *A Retelling in Prose*

William Shakespeare's Cymbeline: *A Retelling in Prose*

William Shakespeare's Hamlet: *A Retelling in Prose*

William Shakespeare's Henry V: *A Retelling in Prose*

William Shakespeare's Henry VIII: *A Retelling in Prose*

William Shakespeare's Julius Caesar: *A Retelling in Prose*

William Shakespeare's King John: *A Retelling in Prose*

William Shakespeare's King Lear: *A Retelling in Prose*

William Shakespeare's Love's Labor's Lost: *A Retelling in Prose*

William Shakespeare's Macbeth: *A Retelling in Prose*

William Shakespeare's Measure for Measure: *A Retelling in Prose*

William Shakespeare's The Merchant of Venice: *A Retelling in Prose*

William Shakespeare's The Merry Wives of Windsor: *A Retelling in Prose*

William Shakespeare's A Midsummer Night's Dream: *A Retelling in Prose*

William Shakespeare's Much Ado About Nothing: *A Retelling in Prose*

William Shakespeare's Othello: *A Retelling in Prose*

William Shakespeare's Pericles, Prince of Tyre: *A Retelling in Prose*

William Shakespeare's Richard II: *A Retelling in Prose*

William Shakespeare's Richard III: *A Retelling in Prose*

William Shakespeare's Romeo and Juliet: *A Retelling in Prose*

William Shakespeare's The Taming of the Shrew: *A Retelling in Prose*

William Shakespeare's The Tempest: *A Retelling in Prose*

William Shakespeare's Timon of Athens: *A Retelling in Prose*

William Shakespeare's Titus Andronicus: *A Retelling in Prose*

William Shakespeare's Troilus and Cressida: *A Retelling in Prose*

William Shakespeare's Twelfth Night: *A Retelling in Prose*

William Shakespeare's The Two Gentlemen of Verona: *A Retelling in Prose*

William Shakespeare's The Two Noble Kinsmen: *A Retelling in Prose*

William Shakespeare's The Winter's Tale: *A Retelling in Prose*